DEADLY SHOWDOWN

———————— ✶ ————————

During another burst of lecherous laughter, Calhoun cocked the shotgun. He drew in a deep breath and let it out slowly. As he stepped out into the open, a cruel smile began to spread across his face.

Before he had taken four steps beyond the horses, Calhoun fired both barrels of the shotgun. Two bandits died, their backs shredded by buckshot.

By the time the three others began to react, Calhoun had one of his Dragoons out. He fired smoothly, evenly, as he walked. Two more of the bandits—including Sepulveda—died, bullets in their chests. Calhoun turned toward the last, ready to blast that bandit into oblivion, too.

ALSO BY CLINT HAWKINS

SADDLE TRAMP
THE CAPTIVE
GUNPOWDER TRAIL
GOLD AND LEAD

Published by
HarperPaperbacks

SADDLE TRAMP

BANDIT'S BLOOD

CLINT HAWKINS

HarperPaperbacks
A Division of HarperCollinsPublishers

HarperPaperbacks *A Division of* HarperCollins*Publishers*
10 East 53rd Street, New York, N.Y. 10022

Cover illustration by John Thompson

First printing: May 1993

Printed in the United States of America

HarperPaperbacks and colophon are trademarks of HarperCollins*Publishers*

❖ 10 9 8 7 6 5 4 3 2 1

CHAPTER

* 1 *

Wade Calhoun rolled out of his blankets, one of his Colt Dragoons in hand, and stared into the blackness of the half-hour just before dawn. He had no idea what woke him; only that someone or something was out there.

He sensed more than actually heard or saw anything in the pitch of the cool night. He closed one eye to preserve his night vision. His Dragoon spit fire into the darkness once. He dove to his right, landing on his bedding, then rolled twice more, coming to his feet. He had been involved in deadly business too long to stand there in the dark after having given away his position with a bright muzzle flash.

As the powder smoke drifted in a lazy cloud around his shaggy-haired head, Calhoun heard a slight whisper of sound. He swung silently in that direction, thumbing back the hammer of the Dragoon as he did. The gun made only the barest of sounds, since it was so well cared for. His horse nickered, and Calhoun knew for sure now that someone was trying to get the animal. He heard another whisper of cloth, or maybe it was buckskin, brushing against foliage, and he fired twice in the direction of the sound.

Just as he pulled the trigger for the fourth time, something hit him a powerful blow in the chest. He fell, twisting toward the side, his shot going well wide of where he had planned it. He heard a crashing in the brush, like a man—or animal—dying.

Calhoun was more than a little surprised there was so little pain. He had been wounded, and badly, before, and there was always an initial pain, followed by a brief time of feeling nothing, before the real pain set in again. This did not feel like any of those times though, and he wondered about it.

He couldn't worry about it, though. There were Indians—at least he assumed they were Indians—out there trying to steal his horse. Considering where he was, he figured they were Apaches. He didn't know much about those Indians, but he had heard enough from men who had dealt with them, usually violently, to know that they were a formidable enemy.

Calhoun pushed himself up, still surprised that he felt no pain, though he was conscious of the arrow still sticking out of his chest. He heard another noise and fired the last shot from his Dragoon. Though the pistol was a six-shot revolver, he, like most men who knew and respected firearms, kept only five chambers of the cap-and-ball revolver loaded for safety's sake. It was one of the reasons he carried two of them.

As soon as he fired, he dove to the right again. He felt the arrow shaft snap as he hit, but he gave it no thought. He rolled until he banged into a boulder. He slid behind the stone and dropped the Dragoon into his holster and pulled the other. Then he waited in the darkness.

He suddenly heard horses crashing through brush, and knew the Indians were fleeing. Still, he waited for what he figured was a half-hour, not certain that the warriors wouldn't take off a short distance and then sneak back on him. The whole while, he had his big, heavy pistol in hand, and worried about the arrow in his chest, and why it didn't hurt like it should. He was not afraid of dying; in fact, he felt just about the opposite. He knew he had been courting death for years now. Only a deep-rooted sense of self-preservation had kept him alive. He might want to die, but he was not about to commit suicide, even if that meant letting someone else do it.

Once, he tentatively touched the broken shaft of the arrow. The thing wiggled fairly loosely, but he was wary about just pulling it out. If he was wounded, it might be that the arrow was stanching the flow of blood. He decided to wait a little longer.

He also wondered about the attackers. He still believed they were Indians, and most likely Apaches, but they could be Mexican bandits, he supposed. It was unlike any Indians to attack at night, as far as he knew, and he had heard that Apaches never did that. Still, he figured, a quiet stealing of a man's horse shortly before dawn might not be out of the question. He shrugged mentally. He would know eventually, he realized, and all the thinking in the world would not give him the answer.

Calhoun squatted behind the boulder until a dull

gray tinged the sky. It wasn't very bright, but it gave off enough light to see some by.

He stood to his full five feet ten. Without fear, he looked down at his chest. Then he laughed, a deep, rich sound. After it had run its course, he thought about it for a moment, realizing that it had been years since he had laughed at all, over anything. Not since before that Sioux raid on the farmstead back in Kansas Territory, and Lizbeth and Lottie had . . .

He pushed that thought out of his mind right away, the momentary bout of humor subjugated by the pain of his loss. The bitterness and deep self-hatred returned with a burst that almost took his breath away. It was some moments before he could settle himself. He uncocked the Dragoon, made sure the hammer rested on the empty chamber, and then slid the weapon away.

He looked down at the arrow again and almost smiled. All these years he had been risking his neck, half hoping for the peace of the grave, but he had god-awful good luck at avoiding that. In all other ways, his luck was as poor as an Indian captive's.

Calhoun grabbed the stub of the shaft and yanked. He nodded his head in wonder as he stood with the arrow in hand. *Of all the piss-poor luck I've had,* he thought, *this's got to be among the worse. Damn.* He dropped the arrow into the dust and scrub grass at his feet.

He pulled the big Bowie knife out and looked at the horn handle, still shaking his head in wonder. He wore the knife in a sheath that dangled from his shoulder a little under his left armpit. The arrow had gone through the Bowie's hilt, partly from the side, then through the pouch of tobacco and the package of wheatstraw rolling papers in his left shirt pocket.

He gingerly pulled out the damaged pouch and papers and rolled a cigarette. There was nothing he could do about the damage to the papers, though he smoothed out the rip in one of them before pouring in the tobacco. He carefully folded the bag of tobacco on itself before stuffing it back into the pocket. He stuffed the tube into his mouth and scraped a lucifer across the stone. He cupped his hands around the match flame against the light breeze and got the cigarette going.

Then Calhoun opened the worn, faded shirt and looked inside at his bare chest. The tip of the arrow-head had barely nicked the skin, sinking in perhaps an eighth of an inch. There was hardly any blood. What there was, he washed away with a bandanna soaked in water from his wood canteen.

Once that was done, he decided he had better see what damage he had caused to the enemy. He figured that if it had been an Indian he had shot, his companions most likely would have carted the body off. Most of the tribes he had dealt with—those on the Great Plains, for a good part—did that.

He pitched the cigarette butt into the remains of last night's small fire and went to his bedroll. Kneeling, he popped the cylinder out of the empty Dragoon, then dredged a new one out of one of his saddlebags and inserted it. He dropped the empty into the saddlebag. He rose and headed toward the brush where he had heard the commotion. Above the spot, turkey buzzards were gathering on the heat currents.

He stopped and stared down at the dead chestnut horse, anger flooding through him. "Dammit all to hell and gone," he muttered.

His poor luck with horses was legendary. It was rare that he was able to get hold of a good one. When he did, the animal was almost invariably lost through violence or being stolen or breaking its leg somehow. He just could never keep a decent horse. Even the nags he often wound up with didn't seem to last him long.

But never once could he remember shooting his own horse by accident. Checking sign in the area, he deduced that when the arrow hit him, it had thrown his aim off, and the ball from the big Dragoon had struck the horse in the head. Calhoun still couldn't believe it.

He checked more sign, and learned that there had been three warriors. He still suspected Apaches; from all he knew, no other Indians were fool enough to cross Apache country. At least not so deep in the heart of their land anyway. He also learned that he had hit one of the Indians, but from the amount of blood he spotted, he didn't think the wound was fatal.

He stood, his pocked face twisted in an angry scowl. Wade Calhoun was not a big man, but he was hard as a pistol barrel and deceptively strong. Cold blue eyes peered out fiercely from beneath the worn slouch hat he had clapped on after reloading his

Dragoon. His face and body were lean and angular, with tough, ropelike muscles cording his arms, neck and legs. He was, altogether, a tough individual, well suited to the land he lived in.

Calhoun's first inclination at seeing the dead horse was to go after the Apaches. That thought fled a-borning, though, since he had enough common sense to know that he would never catch them. If even half of what he had heard about Apaches was true, they would be miles away by now. Even if they weren't, he had heard they could virtually disappear while you were looking at them. He had no love for any Indians, but he was no fool either. He would kill all three warriors the minute he set eyes on them—if he could set eyes on them. Since that was remote, he gave up the thought.

Quietly, he spun and walked slowly back to his camp. He threw some mesquite wood on the fire and fanned the embers with his old hat. Soon flames licked at the fuel and the fire was going well. He stuck last night's pot of coffee near the fire to heat and began preparing some cornmeal biscuits and a small frying pan of bacon and beans. As the food cooked, he poured coffee and leaned back against his saddle. He puffed a cigarette and sipped the thick, mudlike coffee.

He ate without much enthusiasm, and afterward leaned back with another cigarette and the last of the coffee. He wondered for a moment what he should do, but knew he had no choice. He had to push on to Fort Buchanan.

He didn't regret taking on the job of bringing

dispatches to Fort Buchanan from Fort Fillmore. Though Fillmore was three hundred miles or so east of Buchanan, both forts were in New Mexico Territory. And the trail went straight through the heart of Apache lands. Calhoun thrived on challenge, though, and when Colonel Marsh Davidson, for whom Calhoun had scouted some years ago, asked him, Calhoun accepted willingly if not eagerly. He had thought it odd that Davidson was hiring a civilian, even one he knew and had worked with before, for such a job as delivering dispatches. When Calhoun had asked about it, Davidson had explained that he was so short-staffed he couldn't afford to send one of his own men. Since he knew and trusted Calhoun, his problem had been solved.

Calhoun had not had any trouble on the trail until now, which annoyed him more than a little. He had traveled close to three hundred miles unmolested. Now, less than a day's ride from his destination, he had run into trouble.

He figured it would take him two days, maybe three, on foot to get to Fort Buchanan, if he was accurate in figuring where he was. The thought did not thrill him. His boots were worn already, and several days of hiking across the rocks and cactus of this scrubby desert would leave him close to barefoot.

Besides, it was hotter than the back end of hell during the days, even though it was only spring. The nights were often still freezing, though, and the combination served a body poorly.

The only bright spot, he figured, was that at Fort

Buchanan, he should be able to get a horse and some new clothes. Colonel Davidson had paid him for the job, so Calhoun had a bit of cash on him. He rose and began gathering his things, knowing he would get nowhere by sitting around.

It didn't take long. Soon he hiked his fancy Mexican-style saddle up onto his left shoulder. A burlap sack with some food and another with his three small cooking implements dangled from the saddle horn, adding weight to the already heavy saddle. The saddlebags and a special pouch with the military dispatches were tied by leather thongs to the saddle, as was his bedroll.

There was no need to take a last loving look at the campsite. He simply pushed through some brush and back onto the desolate trail that would bring him to Fort Buchanan.

CHAPTER

* 2 *

Calhoun limped across Sonoita Creek and into Fort Buchanan late in the afternoon three days after he accidentally killed his chestnut horse. He was footsore, worn to a frazzle, and not in the best of humor. His clothes were worn out and torn from cactus and paloverde spikes; his boot soles were worn nearly paper thin.

There was no stockade to the fort, just a ramshackle collection of wood or adobe buildings. It looked more like some destitute Mexican village than a United States military fort. Straightening, Calhoun marched directly to the adobe building that served as the commander's office. A sweating, red-faced blot of a private was posted outside the door.

"I got dispatches for Major Muggeridge, Private. Tell him."

"And who're you?" Private Helmut Heydrich asked harshly. There was no trace of an accent, which surprised Calhoun a little. The private looked askance at the dust-covered, perspiring Calhoun. The saddle tramp's razor-thin face was covered with several days worth of whiskers and he looked a fright, even to a poor private stationed in such a desolate post.

"Name's Wade Calhoun."

"Who're the dispatches from?" Heydrich was taking his sentry duty most seriously.

"Colonel Davidson. At Fort Fillmore." Wade Calhoun was a man usually sparing of speech. When he was this hot, tired, and aggravated in general, playing twenty questions with an idiot of a low-ranking soldier brought his temper to a quick boil. It was about there now.

"And what are . . ."

"Tell him I'm here, boy," Calhoun said quietly, but the menace in his voice was unmistakable.

"Yessir." Heydrich spun smartly in an about-face and stepped inside the office.

Calhoun cooled his heels for a few minutes, but that was about all he could stomach. He was standing under the short portico that provided a little shade, leaning against the whitewashed adobe wall. He pushed off the wall, lifted his saddle, and shoved through the door. He caught Major Wendell Muggeridge in the middle of a rant.

Muggeridge slammed to a stop and turned his glittering glare on Calhoun, who had stopped inside and dropped his saddle to the floor. Muggeridge was tall, and not spare of frame. He had billowing bushy eyebrows, matched by mustachios and beard. His uniform blouse was off, and his suspenders were taut across the wide expanse of belly and chest. His white cotton shirt was darkened by sweat in several places. He looked quite imposing, though Calhoun was not impressed.

"What are you doing in here?" Muggeridge

demanded. He was not pleased at the interruption.

"I expect he's already told you that," Calhoun said evenly. He nodded in Private Heydrich's direction.

"Whether he has or not, does not excuse your barging in here."

"You want these dispatches or don't you?" Calhoun asked coldly. He was of no mood to deal with a pompous, overbearing major any more than he was a jerk of a private.

"In good time, my man, in good time." Muggeridge pulled himself out of his chair and turned his baleful gaze on Calhoun. He had tried to sound reasonable.

Calhoun shrugged. "Suit yourself," he said levelly. He jerked the saddle up onto his shoulder, thinking that he was mighty damned tired of carting the thing around. Trouble was, it and his weapons were his most prized, and really only, possessions. He would not be persuaded to give it up.

He turned and headed the few steps to the door. As he got there, he placed his hand on the latch and looked back over his shoulder. "Be advised, though, that your time best come in the next five goddamn minutes or I'll burn the dispatches and haul ass out of here."

"You would not dare!" Muggeridge hissed.

Calhoun grinned at Muggeridge. There was no humor whatsoever in the gesture. He pulled open the door.

"Get in here and deliver those dispatches, you fractious son of a bitch!" Muggeridge bellowed.

Calhoun hesitated, then stopped and looked back

again. "Piss off, Major," he said evenly, then he stepped outside. He turned right and in three swift strides was off the boardwalk and around the corner of the commander's office. He stopped there and leaned back against the adobe wall. He eased the saddle down and rested his right hand on one of the Dragoons.

A few soldiers looked at him curiously. He stared evenly back and the soldiers went about their business.

Just about the time he stopped, he heard the office door open. He peeked around the corner and saw Heydrich stopped and looking around the dusty parade ground. He seemed nervous.

"Lazaro!" Heydrich shouted. A soldier stopped and looked at the private.

"Have you seen that saddle bum who came into the fort a little while back?" Heydrich asked.

The soldier named Lazaro shook his head and continued walking.

"Damn," Heydrich muttered. He mumbled something in German. Imprecations in that tongue increased as he spotted several men stifling chuckles that he knew were directed at him. He drew in a breath and then let it out. Since Calhoun was not out on the parade ground, he must have gone around back of the commander's building. He could not have gotten anywhere else in the few seconds between leaving and Muggeridge ordering him to find the dispatch carrier.

Heydrich shrugged and turned left. He hopped off the end of the boardwalk and looked down the building. No one was there, so he marched down the length of the short building, turned, and went along the back side. He turned the next corner, and stopped, the muzzle of a Colt Dragoon almost stuck in his nose.

"Welcome, Private," Calhoun said quietly.

Heydrich kind of grunted, not being able to form any words.

"I suppose Major Boiled Shirt sent you to find me?"

"Uh-huh."

"Good. Then he must be interested in relieving me of my burden."

"Uh-huh." Heydrich was very scared. He had seen the look in this lean, hard man's eyes; Major Muggeridge had not. Nor was Muggeridge the one standing here with the huge bore of a .44-caliber Dragoon brushing a nostril.

"Now you get the hell back in there and tell that horse's ass that if he wants the dispatches, he's gonna have to come out here and ask for 'em."

"I can't do that!" Heydrich breathed. "He'll hang me."

"You ain't got a choice, boy," Calhoun said flatly. He had spent a number of years around soldiers, and he knew what the young private was feeling. Still, he didn't much care. "You also tell him if he ain't out here askin' for 'em in five minutes that I'll do what I said."

"But . . ."

"Go."

Heydrich felt hugely relieved when the pistol was

suddenly no longer in his face. He lowered his head and stared into Calhoun's icy blue eyes. He knew that Calhoun spoke the truth. The trouble was going to come in convincing Muggeridge of that. Major Wendell Muggeridge was not very open minded, nor was he prone to listening to a lowly private issue an ultimatum from a slovenly gunman. Heydrich knew he was in deep trouble, but he had no choice. He stepped around Calhoun, walked along the side of the building and around the front corner.

He paused just a moment in front of the door to collect himself. Then he pushed open the door and stepped inside.

Muggeridge's bellowing could be heard throughout the post. Some men trembled at the sound; others just smiled, as they would at a noisy thunderstorm if they were inside.

Calhoun strolled out toward the parade ground. He knew he was taking a chance, but he had seen men like Muggeridge before. Such a pompous fool would engender no love from his troops. He was the kind who would prefer to command by bluster and threat, rather than by example. Calhoun figured he was not likely to be shot in the back by someone with an overwhelming desire to preserve Muggeridge's dignity.

He stopped about fifteen yards away from the door, on an even line with it. He set his saddle down, realizing without chagrin that he would be far more apt to be killed by one of these men for the saddle than he was for Muggeridge's honor. He knelt and pulled out the dispatches and made a neat pile of them, as if he were stacking twigs to build a fire. Then he stood.

Slowly, being careful not to spill tobacco through the rip in the wheatstraw paper, he rolled a cigarette. Then he lit it, dropping the still-burning match near the dispatches, figuring Muggeridge might be watching through a slit in the door.

Calhoun smoked the cigarette down. Then he dropped it in the dirt and stamped on it. He could feel its dying heat through the thin soles of his boots. Then he pulled out another lucifer. He held the match a moment, as if studying it. He scratched it across a rough spot on his belt. The sulfur flared.

Cupping the tiny flame against any breeze that might drift along, he knelt and moved the match toward the papers.

The door of Muggeridge's office flew open and Muggeridge himself stepped out onto the wood walk under the portico. "Stop!" he commanded.

Calhoun waited, flames less than an inch from the pile of papers. "Well?" he asked, looking at Muggeridge.

"Deliver those dispatches to me, my man," Muggeridge said in what he thought was a reasonable voice.

"Don't think I heard you right, Major."

"I said, deliver those dispatches to me." He was growing angry, and fighting to control himself.

"Reckon you're just a bit too far away for me to hear you," Calhoun said flatly.

Muggeridge moved a few steps out, until he was away from the shade of the portico, and he repeated his demand, with less patience.

"Match's gettin' mighty short, Major."

"Damn your eyes," Muggeridge snarled. He tromped to a point about halfway between his office and Calhoun. "Give me those goddamn dispatches!" he roared. "Now!"

"Reckon not." The match headed toward the papers.

"Stop!" Muggeridge almost screamed. His face was bright red with choler. He stood there several moments, almost choking. Then, pronouncing each syllable distinctly, he said, "Please deliver those dispatches, as you were assigned to do, Mr. Calhoun."

Calhoun flipped the match. It flew over the papers and landed in the dirt. It sputtered a few moments and then gave up its life. Calhoun scooped up the papers, stuffed them back into the pouch in which he had carried them from Fort Fillmore. He tied the pouch shut and walked to Muggeridge. "Dispatches from Fort Fillmore, with Colonel Davidson's respects," he said. He did not try too hard to keep the sarcasm out of his voice.

Muggeridge grabbed the pouch, glared at Calhoun a moment and then turned away, tramping back toward his office.

A relieved Private Heydrich took up his post near the door again.

Calhoun lifted his saddle and approached Heydrich. "There a sutler's at the fort?"

"In this godforsaken hellhole?" Heydrich asked with something approaching humor.

"I could use some supplies."

"We all could, sir," Heydrich said with new respect in his voice.

"Damn." Calhoun rubbed a hand across the stubble on chin and neck. "There any extra horses about I might be able to buy?"

Before Heydrich could answered, Muggeridge bellowed from inside, "Private Heydrich!"

Heydrich made a face at Calhoun, trying to apologize. Then he was inside. He was not gone long, which surprised Calhoun a little. As he retook his sentry post, Heydrich's face was cloudy with anger. "It is my duty," he started, then added in a whisper, "much as I hate doing it," his voice took up its volume again, "to escort you from the post, sir."

"When?"

"Now, sir."

Calhoun considered for a moment shooting Heydrich or, perhaps better, shoving the soldier aside and storming inside to shoot Muggeridge. Neither would serve him any purpose. He nodded. As they began walking, he asked, "Where's the nearest town?"

"Tubac. It's about twenty-five miles west. Just follow the trail." They walked on a little more, before Heydrich said quietly, "I hope you make it, sir." He paused. "Apaches, you know."

Calhoun glared. "I'll make it," he responded. Then he almost grinned. "Don't know as if I can say the same about my boots, though."

CHAPTER

* 3 *

Calhoun didn't make it too far that day, considering how late in the afternoon it was when he left Fort Buchanan. The more he shuffled onward, feeling every rock and pebble through the thin soles of his worn boots, the more angry he grew at Major Muggeridge.

He knew he had humiliated Muggeridge, and had done so with the full knowledge of what he was doing. So it came as no surprise that Muggeridge had run him out of the fort. Calhoun was certain that Muggeridge had done it in the hopes that Calhoun would run into a war band of Apaches and be killed. Muggeridge struck Calhoun as that type of man.

Calhoun didn't much care. He had traversed three hundred miles of Apache country with only the death of his horse to mar the journey. He figured he could make the last twenty or twenty-five miles to the town Heydrich had called Tubac.

Calhoun didn't really want to stay at the fort anyway. Fort Buchanan was the poorest excuse for a fort that he had ever seen. The buildings were poorly made at best, and there was an air of despair, gloom, and ill health over the whole rickety place. Part of that feeling, Calhoun supposed, came because of its commanding officer, but still, its location seemed unhealthy and terribly isolated.

However, despite not wanting to stay at Fort Buchanan, Calhoun would have appreciated a horse. And maybe new boots, though he could've done without those had he gotten a horse, or even a mule.

Adding fuel to the fire of his anger was the unwelcome feeling that someone was following him. Wade Calhoun was not a man who spooked easily over anything, but the itch between his shoulder blades would not go away. More than once he stopped in the middle of the road, and melted into the thin foliage along the side. There he would watch, silent as a ghost, and listen. Nothing out of the ordinary revealed itself to him on those several occasions, and so he would move on again.

Yet he knew someone was out there. And since he neither saw nor heard anything, despite turning all his trained senses on the world around him, he figured it was an Apache. Or, more likely, a band of Apaches.

The thought both irritated and exhilarated him. He was still irked at the Apaches for trying to steal his horse, which he ended up killing by mistake. He wanted some vengeance for the loss of the horse, as well as the many miles he had been forced to walk since then. Besides, there was the likelihood that he would get a horse. Because of that, he looked forward to fighting a couple of Apaches.

At the same time, he was not fool enough to

desire a run-in with fifteen or twenty battle-hardened Apache warriors.

Dark began to settle over the rocky, rolling land, and Calhoun began looking for a campsite. Half an hour later, he came on a likely spot. As he pulled in behind the thicket of mesquite and began setting up his camp, he finally managed to regain control of his bubbling temper. He still had the itch, and knew that an enemy was near. He would need all his wits about him, and stewing over the insult Muggeridge had dumped on him would do nothing more than get him killed.

He gathered wood and soon had a fragrant mesquite fire going. Then he began cooking up the raccoon he had shot minutes before stopping. He had considered for a second or two before firing whether he should do so or not. Then he realized that however many Apaches were out there knew full well about him. One gunshot wouldn't scare them off, nor did he figure it would bring on an immediate attack.

He was glad now that he had taken the meat since he barely had enough bacon and beans for a meager breakfast. He would hate to have to travel on an empty stomach in the morning. Or worse, fight off a passel of Apaches. As it was, he would have to go real easy on his coffee, having only a cup, or maybe a cup and a half, if he wanted any to get him going in the morning.

His tobacco and cigarette papers were dwindling fast, too. He swore quietly in annoyance at his lot as he waited for the raccoon to finish cooking. When he ate, though, he was grateful for the different meal. He was plumb sick of the usual traveling fare of bacon and beans. He would be glad, too, he thought, to get to Tubac. He just hoped it was in better shape than the fort was. He more than half suspected that it was another little hellhole of a town, like so many others he had moved through over the years. He could expect nothing else out in this isolated desert of rocky hills and cactus-studded flats.

After wiping his meat-greasy hands on his worn, threadbare jeans, he rolled and fired up a cigarette. As he puffed, sipping occasionally from the tin mug of coffee, he felt the tiredness hanging on him like an unwieldy weight. He had been too long on the trail, too many days lately on foot, lugging all his gear. He wanted a soft bed, a hot meal. Most of all, he wanted a hot and soft woman. That, he figured, would restore his spirits.

Darkness was coming fast, and with it a welcome coolness. Gnatcatchers and grosbeaks chirped and chattered in peaceful innocence. It was, Calhoun thought, enough to lull an unsuspecting man into a fatal inattentiveness.

Calhoun leaned back against his saddle, appearing to all the world as a man without a care in the world. He puffed on his cigarette, giving off an aura of unconcern. But his senses were alert.

Gnats and bees hummed through the trees, seemingly in a hurry to finish their day's work and get home. Then Calhoun heard a bird call that was somehow different from the others. A moment later it was answered. Calhoun could not identify how the sounds were different; he just knew it. They were a little distance off yet, but Calhoun knew the Apaches were close. He nodded and threw the cigarette butt into the flames.

He made a great show of rising, stretching, and yawning. He didn't figure the Apaches were close enough to see him yet, but he knew they were in the area, and he wanted to appear completely unsuspecting. He finally spread out his bedroll. Rubbing his scruffy face, he pulled off his boots and then his shirt, working the garment off around the Bowie knife in the shoulder harness. He settled into the bedroll, pulling the canvas and blankets around him.

Then he waited, hand on one of his Colt Dragoons. It took some effort to keep from falling asleep as the last lingering rays of sun burned pinkish red through the shade of the mesquites.

As the shadows lengthened and deepened, Calhoun eased the covers off and slithered out of his bed. Coming into a crouch, he pulled one of his Dragoons and scuttled off as silently as he could toward a dense cluster of creosote bush. He squatted there, once more fighting off the fatigue.

Calhoun half hoped that he had heard right when someone had said Apaches did not attack at night. If it were true, they would either attack any minute, which was good, since it would be over before long. Or it could mean they would not attack until about dawn, in which case he would have a long sleepless night.

Just before full dark covered the small camp,

they came. There were three of them; short, squat, powerful-looking figures as dark as the shadows that spread under the mesquite. They moved like ghosts toward Calhoun's bedroll.

Calhoun, watching them, was a little amazed. The warriors seemed somehow unreal to him. One moment the camp was empty, the next these three inky silhouettes were gliding like the wind across the dirt. Calhoun almost suspected that if he blinked, they would not be there when he opened his eyes.

Still, he was not so amazed at their silent rush that he was incapable of action. He thumbed back the hammer of his Dragoon smoothly and fired five times. All three warriors went down in sprawling heaps.

Calhoun dropped the empty Dragoon into a holster and pulled the other, all the while watching the warriors. He was not about to just walk out there and take a look at the Indians. There might be, he suspected, more of them out in the brush somewhere. Besides, it would not be unthought of for at least one of the warriors to be playing possum, just waiting to draw him into a death trap.

He did slide to the side, trying not to step on rocks, sharp twigs, or cactus, seeing as how he had only socks on his feet. But he did not want to stand where he had been. If there were other Apaches about, or if one of those on the ground was feigning death, they would know where he was—or at least had been—from the muzzle flashes of his pistol. It would give them something to fix on.

He stopped ten or fifteen feet to his right, behind a short, stubby catclaw acacia tree, and he waited.

Whatever moonlight there was had a hard time finding its way into the camp, through the tangle of mesquite, acacia, and various cactuses. The only light in the camp came from the fading orange fire. Even that dimmed almost to nothingness after a while.

When it did, Calhoun stepped cautiously around the acacia's curved thorns, and padded silently toward the three prone figures. A little starlight spread a dim glow over the camp. Not enough to see more than a few inches away, but he should be able to tell if the Apaches were dead when he was kneeling over them.

He squatted by the first and grabbed the dirty mass of black hair in his hand. He tugged the head up. There was no question the warrior was dead. He dropped the head, which kicked up a puff of dust when it hit the ground.

Calhoun eased his way up to the next sprawled figure. He knelt and grabbed the hair.

The Apache jerked himself up, slashing out with something. Calhoun didn't know what the warrior had in his hand, nor did it matter. He figured only the normal action of falling backward under the suddenness of the attack had saved him from a severe injury.

Calhoun landed on his back, one leg half bent under his buttocks. "Damn," he muttered as he got his hands on the dirt and crab-walked backward.

The Apache got up as far as a crouch and then

flung himself at Calhoun. The saddle tramp dropped his pistol and got his hands up in time to catch the flying Apache. He rolled partly onto his side, shoving out with his arms. The warrior hit and grunted.

Calhoun got up, rage flaring hot and white inside his lungs. All his hatred of Indians, born in the fires of a raided Kansas Territory farmstead, surged up in his chest, constricting him. "Goddamned stinkin' red son of a bitch," he snarled. He slid his Bowie knife out as the Apache got unsteadily to his feet. The Indian also had a knife in hand.

The Apache looked like he was having trouble standing, and somewhere in his fury-besotted mind, Calhoun realized that the warrior was wounded, probably badly. But that thought never filtered through to his consciousness. Even if it had, he would not have cared. He had one thing and one thing only on his mind—killing Indians.

The Apache drew in a deep breath, then pulled himself straight. He spit an epithet in Apache, which Calhoun could not understand. Calhoun shrugged and charged.

It was over in moments. With his strength, his speed, and his all-encompassing rage, Calhoun simply overpowered the Apache in the first rush. His left hand shot out, blocking the Apache's feeble attempt to stab him. In the blink of an eye, Calhoun sank his Bowie hilt-deep into the warrior's guts.

For a few seconds, he held the dying Apache up, mainly on the broad knife blade. Then he pulled the knife free and let the Indian fall in the dirt.

Still enveloped by blood lust born of hatred, Calhoun

stalked forward. He was not about to take another chance with this Indian. He walked up, knelt on the warrior's back, jerked his head up in one hand, and ran the razor-sharp blade smoothly across the Apache's throat.

He stood and spun, eyes feral. The third Apache still lay where he had been. Just to make sure he was dead, though, he did the same on that one as he had just done on the other.

Once that was done, the rage roaring in his blood began to subside. He wiped the knife on the back of one Apache's cloth shirt and slid it into the sheath. Then he went and found his pistol. He brushed the dirt off it and checked to make sure none of the caps had fallen off. He dropped it into the holster. Then he loaded the empty Dragoon.

CHAPTER

* 4 *

There had to be horses. Calhoun was absolutely certain about that. The trick was to find where the Apaches had hidden the animals. Calhoun still did not want to go stumbling around in the dark scrub brush, since he was still not sure there weren't some other Apaches lying in wait. Yet he had to find those horses. He was plumb tired of walking, and a horse would make life so much easier.

He walked to his bedroll, sat, and tugged on his boots. Just in case, though, since he did not want to advertise his whereabouts every moment, he pulled off his spurs and tossed them with a quiet jingle onto the blankets next to him. He rose.

Not sure of where to start, he just started walking east and a little north. He figured the Apaches had come from the east, and they would not have been moving on the road. He had an equal chance of being wrong, but he had to start somewhere, and that was as good a direction as any.

Once past the twisting entrails of the mesquite thicket, the moon and stars provided some light. Not nearly enough, but it helped him avoid some of the worst of the obstacles in his way. Taking a leg full of cactus thorns would not be fun out here.

He stopped every few seconds and listened. If there were horses—and, dammit, there had to be, he said silently a dozen times in five minutes—they would make some sort of sound sooner or later.

Eventually one did, and Calhoun almost smiled. He angled to his left, heading in the direction of the sound. He still moved slowly and cautiously, halting briefly now and again to probe the vicinity with his senses.

The sour smell of horse urine wafted over him on the cool night breeze. He was close now, and he began to relax. Before long, he figured, he would be mounted and riding tall. He eased up on the four horses. And then he froze five feet away from them.

The words burned into his brain. Four horses! Four! But there had only been three bodies.

He did not have long to worry about it. Someone slammed into his side and smashed him to the ground. Hard, stubby, callused fingers groped for his eyes, or his throat, or anything else.

"Shit, dammit," Calhoun snarled. The attack had surprised him, which rekindled his rage. That the sudden attack had spooked the horses made him all the more furious. One snapped its tether and ran off. Moments later, the others followed.

Calhoun was too busy to mind it now, though. He fought like a madman, countering every move the Apache made and giving out at least as good as he got.

He finally managed to fling the Apache off him. The Indian hissed when he rolled into a patch of prickly pear cactus.

Calhoun staggered to his feet, breath rasping harshly in and out. He watched with narrowed, hate-filled eyes as the Apache gingerly managed to do the same a few moments later. He, too, had trouble breathing. Calhoun figured the warrior was some-what uncomfortable, covered now as he was with cactus spines. Calhoun was unmoved by the thought.

"Stupid bastard," Calhoun snapped.

The Apache said something in his guttural tongue. Calhoun spit in return. Then the Apache charged.

Calhoun did not hesitate. He jerked out one of the Dragoons and fired twice. The .44-caliber balls slammed the Indian straight up and then drove him back a step. He fell.

Calhoun began putting the revolver back into the holster. Then he remembered the horses running off. In the dead silence of the night, he could hear the faint drumming of their hooves echoing off the ridges of the nearby Santa Rita Mountains. He would never find the animals again. The thought of more walking was not a pleasant one.

The anger flared anew. "Bastard," Calhoun said. He stepped up alongside the warrior and fired a bullet into his head. Then he spun and walked back to his camp.

Angrily he dragged the three bodies there off a ways, not wanting to be disturbed by busy scavengers. He went back to his bedroll and sat. He took the time to clean his pistols properly. All the while, his rage bubbled just below the surface.

When he finished that, he rolled a cigarette, husbanding the tobacco as best he could, and smoked it.

He finally tossed the cigarette butt into the fire and stretched out on his bedroll and pulled the covers around him. Calhoun adjusted himself so he was half on his left side. That would leave his right hand free to go for one of the two Dragoons he wore in cross-draw holsters on the front of each hip, should he need it. It also kept him off his backup gun—a Colt Walker with the barrel cut down to two inches. The short pistol, tucked into a handmade holster at the small of his back, was so packed with powder that the balls barely fit into the cylinders. At close range, it was a devastating weapon.

He took the precautions since he knew damn well there was still a chance that other Apaches were lurking about.

Head resting on his saddle, Calhoun fell asleep almost immediately.

He did not feel much rested when he woke in the morning. Fighting the irritation, he stoked up the fire, put the small coffeepot on to heat the remainder of last night's coffee, and then splashed a little water from his canteen on his face.

Without enthusiasm, he cooked up the last of the bacon and beans. He took the few minutes that the meal needed to cook to smoke a cigarette. Then he cleaned up, packed his few belongings, and trod off down the trail.

About midmorning, he heard a rumbling behind him. He pulled off the trail, not hiding but wanting to give the wagon—for such he thought it was—room to pass.

As he watched up the slightly curving road that went up and down the grass-covered ridges, he spotted the cloud of dust first. Then the wagon hove into view. Two soldiers sat on the seat on the small, short-sided farmer's type wagon. Two other soldiers sat in the flat bed, Calhoun noticed as the wagon drew nearer.

One of the two men on the seat saw Calhoun, and pointed, leaning over to say something to the driver. Calhoun noticed that the driver was Private Lazaro, whom Private Heydrich had spoken to on the parade ground yesterday while looking for Calhoun.

The wagon creaked to a halt, and dust swirled around the occupants and Calhoun for a few moments. Harness leather creaked and the trace chains jingled as the horses shook their shaggy heads.

The sergeant on the seat next to Lazaro looked down at Calhoun and nodded. "That your handi-work back there a ways?" he asked.

Calhoun nodded.

The sergeant grinned. "Good. Goddamn Apaches. Should be kilt whenever ya see 'em." He paused to spit tobacco juice. "Din't ya get one of their horses?" he asked, squinting questioningly at Calhoun.

"All of 'em run off," Calhoun said sourly.

The sergeant nodded in understanding. "Y'all need a ride somewhere, boy?" he asked.

"Wouldn't hurt none to get off my feet."

"I'm Sergeant Wallace. Toss your gear in and climb up with Rodgers and Milkwood back there." He jerked his thumb over his shoulder toward the rear of the wagon.

"Obliged." As Calhoun threw his saddle into the wagon bed, he had the momentary thought that the soldiers would suddenly bolt, taking his saddle and gear. Then he shrugged mentally. If they did, Calhoun knew for certain that he could shoot down Wallace and Lazaro, which most likely would make the wagon crash. Then he could leisurely take care of the others. He was sure of that, too.

Lazaro sat waiting patiently, though, with Wallace beside him watching Calhoun pull himself up next to the two privates identified as Rodgers and Milkwood.

As soon as Calhoun had settled his rump on the rough wood, Wallace nodded at Lazaro. "Ride on, boy," he said after spitting a fair good spray of tobacco juice over the side.

Lazaro snapped the reins, and the two big mules lurched against their harness. The wagon moved into a good pace, and Calhoun settled back to enjoy the ride. He half dozed, swaying comfortably with the jolting roll of the wagon, rousing himself whenever he felt the wagon's movement change. His eyes would pop open, and he would see what caused the change, then drift back into welcome dozing.

He had no great desire to see the countryside. He'd seen deserts before, many worse than this one. Indeed, what little he had seen while he had been walking had been rather pleasant. It was far more green than he expected in a desert. The grass was short but fairly plentiful, and there were numerous different kinds of cactus as well as scrubby brush. Small mountains rose in almost all directions, with low hills rippling elsewhere.

Calhoun thought he might be happy in such an area, but there was always the heat. It was not quite summer yet, but the temperatures during the day were unbearable. A man could break out in a sweat sitting in the shade. It was another reason he hated walking lately.

About three hours after the soldiers picked him up—Calhoun judged it to be just before noon—the wagon slowed.

"Tubac's just ahead, sir," Milkwood said, pointing. He was about nineteen, Calhoun suspected, but a young nineteen. There was an air of innocence about the young man.

Calhoun bent a little back over the sidewall of the wagon and looked ahead. He could see a muddy brown village on the other side of a meandering, shallow stream. As the wagon bounced across the water, Milkwood said, "The Santa Cruz River."

Calhoun nodded.

Minutes later, they pulled into Tubac. Lazaro brought the wagon to a stop in front of an adobe building. A brightly painted sign pronounced it to be Docker's and Meyers' Mercantile.

Lazaro tied the reins around the brake handle and hopped down. Wallace was standing on the dusty street. He spit more tobacco and looked at Calhoun. "End of the line, friend."

Calhoun was already on his feet. He leapt easily over the side of the wagon, landing lightly. He reached back inside and grabbed his heavily laden saddle. With it over his shoulder again, he turned. "There anything like a hotel here?"

"Not a real hotel," Wallace said. He scratched his crotch and looked around. It was evident from the look on his face that he had little liking for Tubac. Too many Mexicans for his taste. It did not alter his opinion one whit that less than three years ago this was still part of Mexico. Even worse, there were too many Indians, peaceful, farming, poor excuses for Indians, no less. He hated the domesticated Pimas and Papagos even more than he did the ferocious Apaches. At least with the Apaches, you could expect a good brawl once in a while, even if they were animals.

"Any place to stay?"

"Many of these folks," he barely kept the contempt out of his voice, "take in travelers and such. Ask here at the store, or in one of the saloons." He refused to call them cantinas.

"Obliged for the ride," Calhoun said. He strolled off, right now desiring the comfortable warmth of a saloon—and its sour smell of old whiskey, beer, and trouble—to the sterile serenity of a general store.

With an unerring sense of precision, he walked straight to a cantina. Even if there was no sign, Calhoun could always pick out a saloon. He wasn't quite sure how he did it, and he never really bothered to think about it. He accepted it as some form of inner compass.

He pushed open the warped wood door and stepped inside. He felt right at home.

CHAPTER
* 5 *

Calhoun walked to the bar, which was simply an old outhouse door, half moon and all, nailed to two large sawhorses. There were no bottles evident. The bartender—a short, smiling, mustachioed Mexican—simply dipped his ladle into a barrel of whiskey and poured that into any one of the odd assortment of dirty cups, mugs, and glasses he had spread out on the bar in front of him.

"This shit drinkable?" Calhoun asked, pointing to the barrel.

"*Sí, sí,*" the bartender said agreeably. "Ees mescal. The best." His head was moving up and down like a cork bobbing on a stretch of white water.

Calhoun was certain the man was lying; that the mescal would taste like it had just passed through a mule after being aged for all of perhaps an hour. However, he really didn't give a hoot. Not now. He hadn't had a snort since he had left Fort Fillmore almost three weeks ago.

The bartender had already scooped up a dose for him and was holding the cup in one hand. His other hand was out, waiting for some money to appear in it.

Calhoun had no problem with that. The man was selling a product and expected to be paid for it. Calhoun obliged the man and took the cup. He turned and surveyed the place. There were six tables crammed into the cantina. Three of them were occupied. Most of the men ignored him, either through fear or simple disinterest.

Calhoun walked to another table, set his cup down, eased the saddle to the floor, and sat with some relief. He downed half the tin mug of whiskey. It was as foul as he had expected, but it still burned a comfortable trail into his gullet.

He rolled a cigarette and lit it. He had enough tobacco left for one more. Unhurriedly, he smoked and sipped. When he had finished, he got a refill on the mescal and then rolled his last cigarette. Finally, he rose. *This is getting to be a pain in the ass,* he thought as he hefted his saddle again. He walked to the bar. "There a place I can bed down a couple days?" he asked.

"Señora Alvarez has rooms," the bartender, Tómas Hildago, said.

"Where?"

Hidalgo turned and shouted a rapid-fire burst of Spanish. A moment later a boy of about nine appeared from behind a blanket curtain that screened a small room off the barroom.

"Sí, Papa?" the boy asked.

Hidalgo issued some instructions to the boy, then looked at Calhoun. "My son will take you there."

Calhoun nodded and handed Hidalgo a coin. "Thanks."

The boy took Calhoun along several streets until they came to a ramshackle adobe house and knocked. A moment later a short, round, gray-haired woman appeared at the sagging door. The boy spoke to her in Spanish. She nodded and answered in the same language.

"Come in, señor," the woman finally said.

Calhoun nodded. He turned and yelled, "Hey, boy." The youngster, who had been running off, skidded to a stop and looked back, suddenly afraid. Calhoun flipped him a copper coin.

"*Gracias, señor*," the boy said happily before heading off at a run again.

Calhoun entered the house. He was enticed by the smells of spices and herbs, of warm, new foods he had never experienced.

The room Señora Alvarez offered was small and close, but more comfortable than Calhoun was used to these past several weeks, and much of his other time as well. It had a straw-tick bed covered by a handsome, soft quilt. A sagging chair and a small table on which sat a long, thin candle in a simple wood holder were crammed against one adobe wall. There was also a thin, short bureau on which there was a basin and a pitcher. The four pieces of furniture took up the vast majority of the room's limited space.

"You like it, señor?" Señora Alvarez asked.

Calhoun dropped his saddle in one corner and turned to Señora Alvarez. "It'll do," he responded. He could tell by the look on her face that she was in desperate need of filling the room to bring in some hard cash. It wasn't that he was being expansive. He needed a place to stay and this was as comfortable a one as he had seen in weeks. Even the religious icons that were omnipresent in the room were not enough to turn him away from it now.

"*Bueno*," Señora Alvarez said with relief. She

paused, then asked with a girllike shyness that was out of place in the thick, matronly body, "How long will you stay, señor?"

"You eager to be shed of me already?" Calhoun asked, making one of his rare—and always feeble—attempts at humor.

"Oh, no, no, señor!" Señora Alvarez said, aghast.

"It was but a poor joke, señora." He knelt and pulled a pouch out of his saddlebags. "I reckon I can use the place a week, if that's all right with you?" he asked as he stood. He extracted a coin from the pouch and handed it to the woman.

"This is too much, señor," Señora Alvarez said, holding the gold coin out. She had a fairly heavy accent, but she was quite understandable.

"Well, maybe I'll stay a bit longer." He paused. "There a place to eat in town?"

"The price of the room includes two meals each day, señor." She wrung her hands together nervously. Many of these Americans did not like the spicy, biting food of northern Mexico. It was why she was desperate to have a boarder. She didn't know how this hard-eyed *Americano* would react.

Calhoun merely nodded.

"Are you hungry now, señor?"

"I am."

"Wash," Señora Alvarez said, waving a pudgy hand toward the basin and pitcher. "It won't be long. I will call you."

Calhoun nodded again, waiting patiently for her to leave. He had nothing against Señora Alvarez, but he felt like a little solitude.

Señora Alvarez stepped out, and Calhoun performed his hasty, not-very-thorough ablutions. He wished he had some tobacco left. Leaving the room, he wandered down the long, dark narrow corridor, following the scent of food to the kitchen.

Señora Alvarez looked up, worry etched on her wide, smooth face.

"There enough time for me to head to the mercantile?" Calhoun asked politely.

Señora Alvarez shrugged. She should have known, she supposed. He wanted to get to a cantina where he could fortify himself against the horrible food he was figuring to be eating soon, she thought. Or else he wanted to down a quick venison steak at the *restaurante*. She sighed. It was always the same for her and her people.

Calhoun wondered what was bothering her. He didn't much care, really, but it always helped to know things about people. It made them easier to deal with. "I don't suppose you got any tobacco to hand, do you, ma'am?" Calhoun asked.

"Ah, *sí*." Señora Alvarez nodded vigorously. She turned toward a cupboard, trying to hide her relief. She pulled out a pouch of tobacco and handed it to Calhoun.

"Papers?" he asked, taking the pouch.

"No," Señora Alvarez said sadly. "Corn husks." A hopeful note sprang into her voice.

"Fetch 'em."

Señora Alvarez did, then went back to her cooking.

"Mind if I just set here, ma'am?" Calhoun asked. It wasn't so much that he wanted company. He just couldn't see going back to that cramped little room to wait.

When Señora Alvarez shook her head, Calhoun took a

seat at the table. As he rolled some tobacco in the thin, crinkly piece of corn husk, he looked around. He was not very familiar with Mexican ways and such, though he was not completely unfamiliar with them either.

An adobe fireplace dominated the room, aided by the beehive *horna* in one corner. Calhoun figured Señora Alvarez had bread baking in the rounded oven. There were several Spanish-style cupboards and a work table against the wall next to the fireplace. Around the room, hanging from the *vigas*, were *ristras* of bright red or blood red chili peppers, long strings of garlic bulbs and others of onions, bunches of green, leafy herbs and vegetables. Fragrant mesquite smoke mingled with the aroma of hot food clouded the room. The kitchen was at one time both exotic in its differentness and yet offering a comfortable homeyness.

By the time he had smoked the cigarette down and stubbed it out under the thin toe of one boot, Señora Alvarez was putting dishes on the table. Calhoun began digging in to the spicy chicken and warm, soft corn tortillas.

Señora Alvarez set a coffeepot down after filling a cup for Calhoun and one for herself. She walked over to her worktable and stood.

Around a mouthful of food, Calhoun said, "You're welcome to join me, ma'am."

Señora Alvarez was startled at the invitation. She knew there was no attraction for her in the offer. He was simply being polite. Still, not too many people came by the Alvarez place these days, and she was pleased to have some company, even a taciturn, gun-toting *Americano*.

She sat on the edge of the old wood chair, ready to leave quickly if she was invited to do so. She more than half expected that. She wanted to speak, but did not know what to say. So she contented herself with sipping her coffee. It was a luxury in which she did not often indulge.

Calhoun finally slowed down in his eating. "Good," he said, sitting back at last. "Or should I say *bueno*?"

Señora Alvarez fairly beamed at the compliment.

"You know anyplace to get supplies?" he asked. He tugged ruefully at his worn shirt. "I saw a place called Docker's and Meyers' Mercantile. That any good?"

"Sí," Señora Alvarez said without enthusiasm.

"There a better place?"

Señora Alvarez took so long in answering that Calhoun had begun to think that she was not going to. Then, slowly, she said, "The *mercado* of old Juan Sosa."

"Why're you against tellin' me?" Calhoun spread some tobacco on a corn husk and rolled it.

"Most . . . Well . . ."

Calhoun stared balefully at her. It had suddenly occurred to him what the problem was. "Doesn't Señor Sosa serve Americans?" he asked calmly. From what he had seen, Calhoun could understand such a feeling on the part of a Mexican businessman.

"He will serve *Americanos,*" Señora Alvarez said. "But most . . . don't want to go there. Don't want to do business with . . ."

"Man sells me what I need, and don't steal me blind in doin' it, I got no problem with him."

Señora Alvarez nodded. "He won't cheat you."

"He have all I need? Clothes, tobacco and such?"

"*Sí.* What brings you to Tubac, Señor . . . ? Señor . . . ?"

"Wade Calhoun." He paused. "Nothin' special brings me here. I brought some dispatches from Fort Fillmore— quite a ways east of Mesilla—over to Fort Buchanan." He scowled. "Commander there asked me to leave the post straight off. I heard this was the closest place around."

"You had no trouble with the Apaches in all that time?" Señora Alvarez asked, eyes wide with surprise.

"I wouldn't say that exactly," Calhoun commented dryly, thinking back to a dead horse and four Apache bodies lying back in the grove of mesquite and acacia.

Señora Alvarez stared at him as a shiver ran up her spine. She was both repelled and attracted by this tall, lean, hard man. She knew such a man would never be attracted to a short, dumpy, graying old woman like herself, but she could always dream. Still, the look in his eyes led her to believe that he was not an easy man to know or grow close to. He was a man, she knew instinctively, who had killed and would do so again. Worse, he would kill easily, if not with pleasure. He was a man well adapted to these wild lands, where death awaited at every turn.

"And now what will you do?"

Calhoun shrugged. He had no purpose in life. Not since he had lost his wife, Lizbeth, and their infant daughter, Lottie. He simply drifted where life took him, taking on jobs when he saw the need and the opportunity. He rested in a place for a bit when he felt the desire; rode on again when that town paled.

CHAPTER

6

Calhoun walked slowly through the dusty streets of Tubac in the gathering dusk. The quiet was broken by occasional bursts of raucous noise from saloons or cantinas. The sun cut through the dust and clouds over the western desert, swathing the brown adobe town in a softening reddish-orangish light. The sunset's gleaming colors did a lot to disguise Tubac's inherent dinginess.

Juan Sosa's small, cramped adobe general store was indistinguishable from the surrounding houses and shops, and it had no sign to identify it. Calhoun found it before long, though, thanks to Señora Alvarez's exact directions.

Calhoun had to give the door a hard shove to open it, since it stuck. Then he entered the store. Several smoky, high-smelling lanterns provided a dull, harsh light. Calhoun was astounded by the mess of goods in the place. The heavy odors of hot spices, leather, wool, and adobe assaulted his nostrils. There was a barely discernible trail that meandered through the haphazardly stacked piles of blankets, clothes, cooking pots, tack, mining equipment, and every other kind of goods a person could want. They reached nearly to the ceiling.

Calhoun followed the erratic track toward a brighter light he could see. The large, single room was close and hot, almost overpowering in its presence. Calhoun finally eased into a small open spot, feeling as if he had just come out of a tunnel. The counter was made of old, weathered planks resting atop two massive kegs. On it sat piles of various foods, jars of tobacco and spices, and a stack of hats.

There were only three people besides Calhoun in the store: a spare, white-haired elderly Mexican man, whom Calhoun assumed was Juan Sosa himself; a homely, pudgy young Mexican woman; and a medium-size, broad-shouldered Anglo man.

The Anglo man had the woman practically pinned against the makeshift store counter. His face was mere inches from hers, and his body almost rested against the woman's. He was fingering her long, wavy black hair.

The man looked over his shoulder as he heard Calhoun's spurs stop. Then, as if certain that another Anglo man would not disturb him in his brutish courting of the young woman, he turned his attentions back to her.

"Please, señor," Sosa said plaintively. His thin white mustache wriggled in agitation. "Leave her alone."

"Mind your own business, old man," the Anglo said.

"But Señor Wilson," Sosa pleaded, "Señorita Luna is a good girl." His voice was heavily accented, but plainly understandable to Calhoun.

Wilson grinned lasciviously at the woman. "This

ain't your concern, you damned meddlin' greaser. Besides," he added, running a filthy finger down one of the woman's plump cheeks, "little missy here is enjoyin' herself. Ain't ya, darlin'?"

Calhoun could not see the man's face, but over the man's shoulder he could see the woman's. There was no way she could be described as showing enjoyment for Wilson's lecherous attentions.

Still, Calhoun did not figure this was his business, so he kept his mouth shut while Wilson continued to paw rudely at the woman and Sosa ineffectually tried to stop the bull-necked Lothario.

The woman was close to tears, but she bit her fleshy lower lips to keep them from brimming over. She was frightened, and that was reflected in her deep, dark eyes, but she seemed determined not to give her accoster the satisfaction of seeing her break down. Calhoun respected her considerably for that.

Still, Calhoun did not think it his place to interfere. He did not know the woman. He doubted it, but for all he knew, the two were really sweethearts having a spat. Interfering in other folks' business usually led to trouble, and Calhoun was not looking for trouble.

Calhoun had little patience even in the best of times, though, and he was not about to stand here all day waiting for the scene to play itself out. He had no real intention of interfering, but he didn't want to just cool his heels while this thuglike Lochinvar pitched his version of woo.

Calhoun stepped up behind the man and tapped him on the shoulder. "Excuse me there, pal," he said quietly.

Wilson turned piggish, bloodshot, irritated eyes on Calhoun. "Get the hell away from here, mister. I don't brook no interference in my personal affairs."

"I can see you're exertin' all your charm on this here young lady," Calhoun said dryly. "But it's distractin' to this old man here."

"Don't mean nothin' to me."

"Nor to me. But I need some supplies, and the old man ain't gonna get 'em for me while he's busy tryin' to stick his snout in your business."

Wilson turned more toward Calhoun. "Well, hell," he said with a touch of exasperation, "you need to convince him of that, not me."

The woman, finding a tad more space between herself and her accoster than before, tried to slide along the counter, away from the man.

"Now just where in hell do you think you're goin', my lady?" Wilson said, whirling back. He slapped a hard hand on the woman's bosom and shoved her back against the counter. Her back bent over the wood, and a small gasp burst from her lips.

Wilson's hand on her chest kept her in the awkward, uncomfortable position. He looked back over his shoulder again. "Now go on about your business, mister. I got my own to tend to." He grinned with an overexaggerated manliness.

The gross grin vanished as Calhoun's stonelike left fist mashed into his mouth. Wilson fell a step to the side, and then backward, hitting the counter and falling off. The pile of hats tumbled after him. A crockery jar fell over, spilling kidney beans all over the sprawled Wilson.

Keeping a wary eye on Wilson, Calhoun held out his left hand toward the woman. "Ma'am," he said quietly.

The woman tentatively took his hand, and Calhoun pulled lightly. She came away from the counter slowly. Fright fought with respect in her eyes as she looked at Calhoun.

Suddenly Calhoun yanked her hard. With a surprised squeal, she stumbled toward him, and he glided a step to the side. She sailed behind him, and he moved back to where he had been, shielding Señorita Luna. One of his Colt Dragoons leapt into his hands.

On the floor, Wilson froze, right hand on his Colt revolver. He had been in the process of drawing it, when Calhoun saw it.

"You got one chance to live, boy," Calhoun said.

"And what's that?" Wilson was scared, and he licked his lips.

"You ease out that pistol and get rid of it. Then you apologize to the señorita here. Hell, you might as well apologize to Señor Sosa, too. Then you crawl out of here."

"I won't do no such . . ."

Calhoun thumbed back the hammer of the Dragoon.

"All right! All right!" Wilson screeched. He was sweating heavily, the perspiration cutting odd little trails through the dust on his face. When he saw Calhoun relax fractionally, he did, too. "I'll apologize to them two, mister, but . . ." He paused to lick his lips nervously again. "But, hell, man, crawl out of here? In front of them?" He pointed a shaky finger at a point somewhere between Señorita Luna and Sosa.

"Why not?"

Wilson's eyes widened with surprise, and he wondered how anyone could be so stupid. "Because they're damned greasers," he said, voice revealing his astonishment that he would have to explain it to a man who obviously had been around some.

"So?" He had no particular love for Mexican people, or any other kind, for that matter. By the same token, he didn't dislike any peoples either—except Indians. He could not abide any Indians since Lizbeth and Lottie had been killed. What he could not understand about men like Wilson or Sergeant Wallace was how they hated any group of people that was not exactly like they were. It baffled Calhoun.

"So?" Wilson echoed, his amazement growing. "So?" He shook his head. If this gun-wielding man didn't know such basic tenets of life—not only here, but throughout the West—Wilson was at a loss to try to explain it to him.

"Make up your mind, boy," Calhoun said evenly. He was tired of waiting. He simply wanted to get his supplies and go on back to Señora Alvarez's. He looked forward to a good night's sleep in a comfortable bed.

He was annoyed, too, at having gotten involved in the first place. He had not intended to do that. Still, his sense of propriety was deeply offended when he witnessed Wilson's treatment of Señorita Luna. He never could abide someone manhandling a woman; couldn't even understand how any man worth his salt could, or would, do that.

"All right," Wilson said. He sounded defeated. He

looked up at Sosa. "Sorry, Sosa," he said with a decided lack of sincerity. "You, too, missy," he added hypocritically. He could not see Señorita Luna.

"Don't sound to me like you meant it, boy," Calhoun said. Over his shoulder he said, "Come on up here, ma'am." When Señorita Luna edged worriedly up to his side, Calhoun said, "Now, make your apologies to the lady here, boy, like you believe what you're sayin'."

Wilson glared at Calhoun, hate undisguised in the dim dots of eyes. Hate also clouded his reason. He began to think that since this lean, hard-looking fellow hadn't shot him yet, he wouldn't. "I've done all the apologizin' to these damned greasers that I'm going to," he said adamantly.

Calhoun fired the Dragoon without reservation. The heavy, .44-caliber ball shattered Wilson's right leg below the knee.

Wilson howled in shock and pain. He could not believe that this man—whatever his name might be—had so casually cost him a leg. His hands darted forward to grab the little bit of whole leg between the wound and the knee. He held on, as if trying to stanch the flow of blood with his hands.

Deep, gnawing fear mingled with the rage. He had been a fool, and he now realized it. He wondered how he could have so misjudged this man.

Wilson sat there, as the waves of anger, pain, and fear swept over him like the rolling of the grasslands. When he thought he had those feelings under control, he looked at Señorita Luna.

The woman was standing there, mouth agape, one soft brown hand covering the orifice. Her eyes were wide as saucers.

"My apologies, ma'am," Wilson said, sounding far more sincere than he had earlier. He reached up with his bloody right hand and touched the brim of his stained hat. When the hand came down, it fell listlessly to his side—near his pistol. Now that he knew just what kind of man he was dealing with in Wade Calhoun, he would do whatever he could to stay alive. He hoped that he might lull Calhoun into relaxing some, and then maybe he could change his situation.

"That acceptable to you, ma'am?" Calhoun asked without looking at Señorita Luna.

"Sí, señor." Señorita Luna was still very frightened, and she remained uncertain of all that was happening here. She had been accosted by Anglo men before, and was somewhat used to it by now. Like many women of Mexican ancestry here in Tubac and places like it, she had learned to accept such insults and not let them annoy her. Still, no one had ever been so persistent in his attentions as Slade Wilson, a sometimes drunk, occasional mine worker, and a full-time bane of Mexican people.

She was grateful for the intervention of this tall, hard stranger, but she wondered if the new one would take up where Wilson had left off, once Wilson was out of the picture. She didn't think that would happen, but one could never tell with Anglos.

Señorita Luna was also rather shocked at Calhoun's remorseless shooting of Wilson. She had seen plenty of violence in her twenty-one years, but never such as this. It wasn't so much the callousness of it, she decided, but rather the definitiveness of it that scared her. A man who could so easily destroy another's leg was capable of considerable mayhem. She really hoped that this newcomer was truly on her side.

"You satisfied with the apology, Señor Sosa?" Calhoun asked.

"*Sí.*"

Calhoun looked at Wilson. "Your leg being in such a condition ought to make crawlin' out of here that much easier," he said easily.

CHAPTER

* 7 *

Wilson started to roll gingerly toward his left, moving to get up onto his left leg. That would allow him to drag the splintered hulk of his right leg along. It would, he hoped, be the least pain-filled way of making his way across the miles of floor that separated him from the small door.

It also would, he thought, give him possible access to the .44-caliber Colt on his right hip. He was fairly certain he would never be able to make it to the door, even if this wild man watching over him permitted it. Wilson knew for sure that he would rather die than crawl all that way in searing agony. Yet, he did not want to die for nothing. He still hoped to use his old Colt.

The thought pleased him. He could envision it. He would start to move, slowlike and racked with pain. Or so it would seem to the pock-faced man standing there watching him with those clear, deadly blue eyes. Once Calhoun was lulled, Wilson could see the old Colt hogleg suddenly appearing in his hand. He could see the round lead balls punching bloody holes in Calhoun's body, making the saddle tramp do an odd dance.

Then, Wilson figured, he would somehow get himself to his feet—well, dammit, foot anyway—and hobble out, upright as a man should. Once he was recovered, he'd come back here and mash old Juan Sosa around a bit. Mostly, though, he would look forward to finishing his business with Señorita Luna. He would enjoy that. He sure as hell would.

"Let's make some progress, pal," Calhoun said with soft menace.

Wilson looked up, terror and pain in his eyes. So immersed in his dream had he been that he had not made more than an inch worth of movement. He groaned and started rolling as softly as he could again, trying not to jostle the remains of his right leg.

Halfway onto his left side, he decided he had had enough. Whether Calhoun was lulled or not, Wilson knew he had to make his move. He could not bear the pain. Nor the humiliation. He flopped onto his back, sweat covering his pasty face. "I can't do it," he moaned.

"You can die right there, if you prefer," Calhoun said casually.

Wilson knew Calhoun was serious, but he found he couldn't care too much. Still, his hand was mighty near to his pistol. He made a great show of sitting up, bending at the waist so as not to jostle his pulsing lower leg.

Just as he made it into a sitting position, his right hand swept out the Colt. Almost.

Wilson's revolver was less than halfway out of the holster when a ball from Calhoun's Dragoon drilled a hole through Wilson's forehead and exploded out the back.

Wilson never even felt it. He was just suddenly flung back onto the floor, dead before the burst back of his skull slapped on the hard-packed dirt floor of Sosa's store.

Silence came to the close confines of the shop, though the cloud of powder smoke took longer to dissipate.

"Oh, señor," Señorita Luna said as she peered around Calhoun's shoulder at the bloody remnants of Slade Wilson. *"Gracias. Muchos gracias."* Señorita Miranda Luna was a protected young woman, one who usually was kept from many of the seamier sides of life. She found herself surprised at her callousness in seeing Wilson's body—and rejoicing in the odious man's death. She didn't care, though. Wilson was a despicable human being, and Señorita Luna was not ashamed to admit that she was glad he was dead.

Señorita Luna made the sign of the cross quickly and whispered a silent, quick prayer for Wilson's soul. She might be glad he was dead, but her religion and its tenets were deeply ingrained in her. Almost absentmindedly, she slid one soft, plump hand around Calhoun's left arm and grasped it lightly, yet firmly.

"Madre de Dios," Sosa breathed. He looked across his counter at the body. Then he offered up a long string of words in Spanish. His speech came in sharp, rapid bursts of agitation.

Calhoun could not understand a single word Sosa

said as he looked at the store owner over his shoulder.
He was well aware, however, that Sosa was dis-
pleased, and was directing that displeasure at him.
He did not know why, though.

Calhoun let Sosa rant on, while he slowly began
reloading the Dragoon. It was difficult with Señorita
Luna still clinging to his left arm, but he didn't want
to disturb her any more than she was. She had come
through a traumatic time, Calhoun knew, and he
could see no good reason to add to her burden by
seeming to reject her.

Finally, though, he was done with his pistol and he
dropped it into the holster. He half turned, looking at
Sosa, who was still at it. The movement shook Señorita
Luna out of her stupor. With a guilty look, she released
Calhoun's arm. She wrung her hands together, as if
worried that she had done something terribly wrong.

Calhoun almost smiled at the woman before turning his attention back to Sosa. He shook his head.
He, too, was agitated by the situation, and he was
becoming more so after five minutes of Sosa's non-
stop babbling.

"Shut up, old man," Calhoun finally snapped, temper
flaring. The words were not loud, but they carried well
nonetheless.

Sosa creaked to a halt, and stood looking dumb-
founded—and extremely worried. The fingers of one
hand drummed nervously on the plank counter.

"You mind tellin' me what was stuck in your
craw?" Calhoun asked.

Sosa began his rambling outbreak of Spanish
again, until Calhoun glared at him.

"English, old man," Calhoun ordered.

"I wish you had not come in here, señor," Sosa said with some hesitation in his voice.

The only sign of Calhoun's surprise at the statement was a slight raising of his eyebrows.

"Well, I am glad he did," Señorita Luna said, a touch defiantly. Then she flushed at her presumptuousness.

"Sí, sí." Sosa nodded unconvincingly. He understood the young woman's feelings, but he did not have to like any of this.

"Then why are you acting this way?" Señorita Luna asked after taking a few moments to get over her surprise.

"There will be trouble over this," Sosa said, his nervousness increasing.

"From who?" Calhoun asked. He doubted any marshal would raise a fuss over the death of a man like Wilson, especially after Wilson's actions toward Señorita Luna.

"El autoridad," Sosa said, something like awe, or maybe it was fear, in his voice.

"Who?"

"The authority," Señorita Luna said for him.

"Who is he?" Calhoun asked. Not that he really cared all that much.

"Señor Madison Goodykoontz." His accent made a mishmash of the name.

"Who?"

Señorita Luna repeated the name. Since her accent was much lighter, the name was understandable.

"He the marshal or somethin'?"

"No, señor," Sosa said, irritation growing again. "There is no *mariscal* in Tubac."

"Then who's the law?"

"Señor Goodykoontz," Señorita Luna said.

Calhoun's temper was beginning to boil again. They had sort of covered this ground before, and he didn't want to go over it again, but he figured he would have to do so at least once more. "And who is this fellow?"

"The head of the Santa Rita Mining and Exploration Company."

"And he runs things?" Calhoun asked.

"*Sí,*" Sosa and Señorita Luna answered in unison.

Calhoun nodded. "What makes you think he'll cause trouble over the death of this trash?" He spit toward the body.

Sosa shrugged, a natural fatalism replacing some of his fear. "I just know, señor."

"I am afraid Señor Sosa is right," Señorita Luna said. She was still grateful Calhoun had saved her; always would be. But she was now worried about what would happen to old Juan Sosa. She hung her head in shame, but then slowly brought it back up. "It is because we are Mexicans, señor." She realized that she still did not know her savior's name.

Calhoun stared at her for a moment. Then he nodded. He should have known it, he thought as the realization crept over him. Ethnic hatred was never far away. Calhoun could feel it lying over Tubac as he had strolled the streets, though he had taken no note of it then.

"Well," he finally drawled, "I reckon there ain't no

reason for this Mr. Goodykoontz to know about any of this." He paused. "There any place I could dump the body so it wouldn't be connected with your place?"

Sosa scratched his long fingernails down one gaunt cheek as he thought. "The arroyo," he finally said.

"Where?"

"It runs east and west near the north edge of town," Señorita Luna said. "It's about two hundred yards from the store."

Calhoun nodded. "Then if you'll excuse me, I got work to do." As he turned toward the body, he added, "Soon's I haul this trash out, you clean up what's left, Mr. Sosa. You do a good enough job, and ain't nobody'll ever know he was here."

"Sí," Sosa said, his face brightening with anticipation.

Señorita Luna stood, biting her heavy lower lip and watching Calhoun. Suddenly she said, "I will lead you to the arroyo, señor."

"Might be dangerous for you."

"I am not afraid." She did not add, though she thought, *I will never be afraid when I am with you.*

Calhoun grunted acknowledgment. He glanced at Señorita Luna when she asked quietly, "Just one thing, señor—what is your name?"

"Wade Calhoun." He knelt beside the body. "You got a canvas sack, Mr. Sosa?" he asked.

"Sí," Sosa said. The aging store owner got the requested item and brought it to Calhoun, who looked it over. Satisfied that it could not be identified with Sosa's store, he pulled the sack over Wilson's head and tied it on. Sosa watched quietly.

Then Calhoun stood, hauling the body with him and boosting it over his shoulder. "After you, ma'am."

Señorita Luna led the way out the side door. Calhoun followed along easily despite his burden. They moved slowly as they passed the last of the houses and reached the desert. It was dark, and the land rocky, broken, and studded with cactus.

Finally Señorita Luna stopped. "Right here," she said.

Calhoun nodded as he halted. He jerked his shoulder and the body tumbled off his shoulder, hit the ground and rolled into the dusty arroyo. Then Calhoun and Señorita Luna walked quietly back to Sosa's store.

The old man had the place pretty well cleaned up. All he had done was dig up the bloodstained areas of the hard-packed dirt floor and flung the dirt haphazardly outside. With the shovel he had moved some other dirt around to fill in the holes, and then stamped that dirt down. Within a few hours of having customers tomorrow, he figured the place would be indistinguishable from when the trouble had started.

"Now, if you don't mind, Mr. Sosa, I'd be obliged if you was to sell me some goods," Calhoun said after Sosa had put his shovel behind the counter.

"*Sí,*" Sosa said, his humor restored. He looked askance at Calhoun, not wanting Calhoun to take his words the wrong way. "What brought you here, Señor . . ." He paused, then asked weakly, "What is your name, señor?"

"Wade Calhoun. I come here at the suggestion of Señora Alvarez. I'm roomin' over at her place."

"Bueno." Sosa felt much relieved. "Now, Señor Calhoun, what can I get for you?"

As Calhoun ordered what he needed, Señorita Luna stood there watching him with interest, rolling his name around in her head, over and over. And, later, after he had escorted her home to ensure her safety, she spoke it aloud, softly. She liked the way his name trickled so easily off her tongue. She wondered what he would be like to be with, just the two of them, in a bed. She flushed hotly as she pulled on her nightclothes.

CHAPTER

8

* *

Calhoun was aware of the man well before the man reached him. He was ready for anything, too, since the man had a mighty determined look about him.

Reese Tate fancied himself a gunman, as well as a man to be wary of. As such, he didn't think he needed to be shy about approaching people. Still, he came at Calhoun obliquely, from the left. He didn't want Calhoun to see him coming straight at him, and possibly hightail it. Reese Tate thought a lot of himself.

Tate didn't know—would never know—how lucky he was to be alive after grabbing Calhoun's left shirt sleeve. Calhoun had one of the Dragoons half out, thumb easing back the hammer. But at the last moment, he stopped the action, figuring there was no need for killing here. Not yet anyway. Still, he vowed silently to give this pest a lesson in civility before they parted ways.

Tate tugged on Calhoun's sleeve a little. "Whoa, hold on there, hoss," he said. He was absolutely sure his tone was reasoned but yet menacing.

Calhoun stopped and glared at the man. He had not heard any threat in Tate's voice. As Tate swung around square in front of him, Calhoun took stock of the man.

Tate was a bit taller than Calhoun, though not as broad of shoulder or thin of waist. He was rather a handsome man, with a smooth, clean-shaven face and pinkish cheeks. A neat butternut shirt and pair of dark blue wool pants covered his spare frame. A bright blue bandanna encircled his neck, the point facing straight down his sternum. A pair of tall black boots and a short, flat crowned hat completed the tidy ensemble.

"That's better," Tate said, nodding his head once in a very precise maneuver.

Calhoun glared balefully from Tate's face to the hand on his arm, then back to the face.

Tate seemed not to notice. "Now, come on with me, pard," Tate said, giving Calhoun's sleeve a sharp tug. "The boss wants to talk to you."

Calhoun was immovable—at least as far as the tugging on his arm. Instead of moving his feet forward, the way the annoying man wanted, Calhoun's right fist snapped out, connecting smartly with the underside of Tate's jaw.

Tate rose up on his toes with the power of the blow, and his hand released Calhoun's shirt in a hurry. He did not go down, though his eyes were glazed for a few moments. He finally shook his head, trying to clear it. He was beginning to get a bit worried, thinking that perhaps he had underestimated this man just a little.

"What the hell'd you do that for?" he asked, trying to keep the whining surprise out of his voice.

"Might teach you to keep your hands to yourself," Calhoun commented with a shrug. "Now get your ass out of my way."

"Can't do that," Tate said, backing up a step. He reached for one of the two walnut-handled Remingtons he wore on his hips.

Calhoun hit him three times before Tate could blink. Two blows mashed his nose and split both lips; the third bruised his forehead and staggered him. Tate went down on his buttocks, eyes dull.

Calhoun considered walking away, but decided almost immediately that he did not feel like letting it end so soon. He did not think the annoying would-be gunman had learned much of a lesson.

So he stepped up and kicked Tate in the chin. It wasn't as hard a kick as he could make, but it was sufficient to lift Tate's rear end a couple inches off the ground, and snap his head back. Tate fell backward. Dust erupted from the impact. Tate groaned.

Calhoun knew that people had gathered and were watching him, but he didn't much care. He never did care about such things, beyond being aware of any possible danger. There seemed to be none here.

"You ought to not pester folks on the street like that, boy," Calhoun said. With the heels of his new boots, he stomped on Tate, breaking several ribs, his right forearm, and his right shin.

Calhoun knelt alongside the moaning Reese Tate. "Y'all can tell your boss that I'll kill you—or the next son of a bitch—he sends after me like that. Understand?"

Tate groaned, but said nothing.

"I asked you a question, boy," Calhoun snapped.

"Yes," Tate hissed. He was in more pain than he ever even imagined possible. He had always seen himself as the winner; the one to cause pain. He could not understand how less than a minute ago he was swaggering up the street, people clearing a way for him, and now suddenly he was lying here staring at the sky, agony racking his body.

Calhoun rose and walked away, continuing the leisurely stroll he had started at Señorita Luna's house. He was heading nowhere in particular; he just wanted to get the lay of the town. He was decked out in the clothes he had bought from Sosa the night before: dark blue cotton shirt, stiff new denims, a pair of serviceable boots that actually had soles and heels, a new slouch hat of the mousy gray color he favored.

He had a bellyful of Señora Alvarez's tamales and coffee, and he was actually feeling pretty good—or as good as he ever felt. At least he had been, until that damn fool had accosted him right there in the street. Calhoun shook his head in anger, wondering how any man could be so dense. You simply didn't come up on a man's blind side and grab him. It wasn't good manners; nor was it a very wise way to go on living.

The incident had soured Calhoun on the otherwise pleasant day. The heat was high, but not too insufferable. A light breeze was blowing, picking up small, scudding dust devils in the dirt streets of Tubac.

He tried to calm himself as he walked, observing

the people. There was something about the Mexican people, of whom there were many, that appealed to him. Especially the women. Maybe it was the soft, smooth duskiness of their skin. Or the relaxed, casual way they generally looked at life. Whatever it was, it translated to a comfortable place, even with the tension between the Mexicans and the Anglos.

There were plenty of Indians in Tubac, too. Mostly Papagos and Pimas, Señora Alvarez had told him that morning over breakfast. These Indians were unlike those he was used to dealing with—the fierce warriors who roamed the Great Plains. The Pimas and Papagos were farmers, and lived a fairly sedentary life. They suffered, Calhoun had learned, even more than the Mexicans or the Anglos, from the depredations of the Apaches. Moreover, they had been suffering those attacks for centuries, Calhoun figured.

Calhoun spotted a saloon and headed toward it. From the outside, it looked like every other building in Tubac—flat-roofed adobe, with an abundance of *vigas* sticking out near the top.

Inside, though, it was far different. It still had the earthiness inherent to the area: adobe walls, heavy wood furniture, packed dirt floor. This saloon, though, had a real bar, carted in from somewhere back east at considerable expense, Calhoun figured. There was no back bar, but the few bottles of real whiskey were stacked neatly in two wood cabinets. The walls were painted a refreshing white, and artworks were hung at evenly spaced intervals. The tables were unscarred by violence and the chairs looked both substantial and comfortable.

Calhoun ambled to the bar, feeling somewhat out of place, not that he would let that bother him. Still, he felt more comfortable in a saloon or cantina like Tómas Hildago's. On the other hand, such a place usually attracted angry, desperate, tough men—men just like him—and such a clientele made a saloon like that dangerous. Here there was a feeling of money, easy respectability. Calhoun wasn't sure he liked that, either.

The bartender, a tall, heavyset man with slicked-back hair and full mustache, was standing at the bar in front of him, waiting patiently. As he did, he wiped his hands idly on his wide white apron.

"You got any rye back there?" Calhoun asked without much hope of it being true.

"Yessir." The bartender was nonchalant. This might not be New Orleans or St. Louis, but they had managed to bring in quite a few amenities. He and his boss were proud of that, though it would never do to show that in public.

"I'll take a bottle, then."

"Yessir." With very precise movements, the bartender turned and opened one of the cabinets. He pulled out a bottle, then carefully closed the cabinet door. He turned and placed the bottle gently on the table. "Twenty dollars," he intoned, without blinking an eye.

"Kind of steep, ain't it?"

"When one wants the best," the bartender said pompously, "one must pay for it."

"You're a goddamn thief," Calhoun commented. He reached into a pocket and pulled out a double eagle. He set the gold coin on the bar and shoved it forward with an index finger. "But I don't figure you're the one settin' the prices." He pulled the finger off the coin.

The bartender picked the money up and moved the bottle closer to Calhoun. He set a glass—a real one, not one of the crockery ones so prevalent around here—next to the bottle. "Enjoy it, sir." Then he was gone.

Calhoun took the bottle and glass in his left hand. He turned and walked slowly toward a table and sat. He poured a drink and sipped it, savoring the rich amber liquid. He couldn't remember the last time he had gotten whiskey as smooth as this. Most of the places he frequented served only the most foul forty-rod.

Time slipped away as Calhoun enjoyed the rich liquor. He paid as much attention to the other customers as they did to him, though he was unobtrusive about it. He was used to being stared at, and while it might be irksome, it meant little to him.

Finally, though, he had enough whiskey for the time being. What he wanted was a woman, but he thought forty winks might be better right now. He jammed the cork into the bottle and left. He was a little grateful that Señora Alvarez was not around when he reached the house and let himself into his room. He did not feel like company—at least Señora Alvarez's company—at the moment.

Wade Calhoun was not a very sociable man. Oh, he had been sociable enough early on, but once Lottie and Lizbeth had died, the light of civility seemed to have gone out in him. He could abide people of a time, but not often, and not for too long at a stretch. Not even kindly, mothering ones like Señora Alvarez.

He crawled into the comfortable bed, thinking as how he could get to like this life if he didn't watch it. Then he fell asleep.

When he woke, he washed up in the basin. He pulled the cork on the bottle and downed a healthy mouthful of rye. Then he corked the bottle again and left, leaving the whiskey on the table. He stopped just outside the adobe house, breathing in the stifling air, as he rolled a cigarette. Scraping a match on the wall, he cupped his hands around it, blocking out the hot, brittle breeze that skittered up the street.

The afternoon gave Tubac a different look than it had had in the morning. The shadow lines of buildings were now more stark, as the harsh edge of the sun cut more sharply. The wind blew in sharp, short gusts, blowing up dust devils and foul odors. The town was quiet, except for dogs occasionally yapping. Many of the Mexicans were taking their siesta; quite a few of the Anglos had gone off to work at the mines a few miles off. The quiet did not imbue a feeling of comfort; only feelings of deadness, danger, and abandon.

Near the spot where he had been accosted before, Calhoun was instantly aware of another man heading toward him, angling from across the street. This one did not sneak or swagger. He simply walked easily up in front of Calhoun and stopped. He stood with his arms at his side, unthreatening.

He was a medium fellow, of average height and weight. Nothing in his looks, clothes, or demeanor would distinguish him from a thousand other men.

Calhoun stopped, facing him and waiting.

"A moment of your time, mister?" the man asked in a pleasant baritone.

Calhoun shrugged.

"Mr. Goodykoontz asks that you stop by to see him, if you're of a mind."

"When?"

"Now would suit Mr. Goodykoontz best." The man did not looked worried.

Calhoun shrugged again. "Won't put me out too much, I expect." He paused. "Lead the way." It was not politeness; it was an order.

The man understood that. He turned and strolled away, not bothering to check to see if Calhoun was following.

CHAPTER

* 9 *

Calhoun was led to the same saloon he had been in before. Instead of stopping in the saloon, though, the man, who had not offered his name, continued through it, and opened a door at the rear of the saloon. He stepped aside, letting Calhoun enter.

The room was simple in its finery. The few pieces of furniture—desk with chair, two other chairs, a full bookcase on which sat several crystal decanters and matching glasses, divan and small table—were of heavy, dark wood. All the pieces were obviously imported. There was no wood around these parts that would make such fine furnishings, no matter how good the workman. Several small, tightly woven rugs covered the floor.

It was the man sitting behind the desk, though, who dominated the room.

Madison Goodykoontz was a large, extremely portly man, whose wide girth, fleshy jowls, and fancy, store-bought clothes belied his strength and ruthlessness. He took pride in cultivating the image of a rich, fat man who was neither strong nor daring. It fooled many people.

Calhoun was not one of them, though. He could

see the coldness in Goodykoontz's deep-set, piercing blue eyes. They were the eyes of a man used to commanding, one not shy about ordering bloodshed and death.

Though Calhoun figured Goodykoontz was only in his mid-thirties, he was mostly bald, sporting only a fringe of short, fair, frizzy hair. Big, soft-looking hands rested on his immense, vest-covered stomach. Goodykoontz had a very small mouth and nose, both of which looked very odd in the big, fleshy face. Combined with an almost complete lack of eyebrows, his face had the look of a crumpled sock.

Clouds of lime water wafted off Goodykoontz, swirling about the room. Calhoun was never much of one for such fancified odors, or people, for that matter.

Goodykoontz waved one of his pale, flabby hands toward the two large, stuffed chairs that faced the desk. "Be seated," he commanded in a soft, almost womanish voice.

Calhoun thought of looking over his shoulder at the man who had brought him here, but then decided that would be foolish. The man had made no move that Calhoun could tell since they had entered the room. Calhoun shrugged and took a seat.

Goodykoontz nodded. He looked toward the door. "Mr. Perlmutter, some brandy for the gentleman. And myself," he added almost as an afterthought.

Harry Perlmutter pushed away from the wall and poured two glasses of brandy from the crystal decanter. He gave one to Goodykoontz, and handed the other to Calhoun. He did not seem put out by the chore.

"A cigar?" Goodykoontz asked.

"Wouldn't hurt none."

"Mr. Perlmutter," Goodykoontz said.

Perlmutter, still standing beside Calhoun, picked up the thick wood box from the desk, opened it, and presented it to Calhoun. The saddle tramp glanced at Perlmutter and still saw no sign of annoyance or overt subservience. Holding the glass of brandy in his left hand, Calhoun pulled out a cigar and sniffed it, savoring the rich, baked earth aroma.

Calhoun bit off the end of the cigar and spit it into the cuspidor near the corner of the desk. He stuck the cigar in his mouth and waited for a light. It was not long in coming, as Perlmutter held out a flaming match. Calhoun soon had the cigar going and was sipping at the brandy.

Perlmutter set the box down near Goodykoontz, and then went back to his post by the door, behind and a little to Calhoun's left. Calhoun held both cigar and glass in his left hand, leaving his right hand free. The hand rested loosely on the upper part of his right thigh, near to the Colt Dragoons, just in case.

He enjoyed the cigar, knowing he had never had one so expensive, and had little chance of ever having another. The brandy, on the other hand, was not to his liking—it was too full-bodied and rich for him. He preferred something with more bite; something that would burn its way into a man's innards, not glide like a smooth pebble down an ice floe. Still, he was not about to complain. He did wonder, though, what this was all about.

"I am Madison Goodykoontz," the fat man said. A faint flicker of annoyance drifted across his pale eyes when Calhoun did not react the way he expected. Goodykoontz's tiny mouth pursed, then relaxed. "Just why did you kill Slade Wilson. Mr. . . . ?"

"Who's he?"

"The man whose body was found in the arroyo north of Juan Sosa's store at first light."

"Never heard of him," Calhoun answered evenly, blowing out a mouthful of smoke. "Why bother me about it?"

Goodykoontz's little pink tongue probed out, roved around the minuscule lips, and disappeared. "We've had no real trouble here in a long, long time, Mr. . . . ?" A bit of irritation crept into his voice at Calhoun's lack of response. "Yes, a long time."

Calhoun was sure Goodykoontz was lying. Trouble was easy to come by in a place like Tubac. There were tensions between Anglo and Mexican, Anglo and Indian, Mexican and Indian. There were several huge mines for which Tubac was headquarters, and miners were not the most genteel of folk. Tubac had God knew how many saloons and cantinas. Apaches roamed the hills and deserts. All of which would breed frequent trouble.

Goodykoontz had paused, awaiting some reaction from Calhoun, which still was not forthcoming. He sighed heavily. "Well, then you come along, and soon after a body turns up."

"Don't mean I had anything to do with it," Calhoun said, unperturbed.

"You were seen leaving that old greaser's store." Goodykoontz's voice had taken on a slightly harder tone.

Calhoun remained unconcerned. "Still don't mean I had anything to do with it." He paused a moment, looking at the glowing tip of his cigar.

"The evidence, circumstantial as it might be, makes me believe that you did have something to do with it." Goodykoontz maintained a peaceful facade, but he was growing increasingly angry.

Calhoun shrugged. "I don't much give a damn what you believe." Again he was speaking only the truth.

Goodykoontz's puffy fingers played a silent tattoo on the wide wool vest as Goodykoontz thought and tried to keep control of himself. It did not pay, he knew from long experience, to let one's emotions rule one's head. Such things brought only trouble.

Finally he said softly, "I suppose Mr. Sosa could be persuaded to tell me who did it." The threat was implicit in his voice, as was his obvious loathing for Mexicans.

"That wouldn't be very neighborly," Calhoun said flatly. "Nor safe," he warned.

Goodykoontz did not like being challenged, but he put the irritation at that aside for now. He was intrigued by this hard-edged man. He might have a use for him. "Do you know who I am, Mr. . . . ?"

"Madison Goodykoontz," Calhoun said dryly. "Unless you were lyin'."

"Hardly." Goodykoontz took a sip of brandy and then entwined his fingers on the broad prairie of his abdomen. Noticing Calhoun's empty glass, he asked, "Would you like another brandy, sir?"

Calhoun shrugged. "You got anything else?" *No harm in asking,* he thought.

"Some bourbon. Rye, I suppose."

"Rye, if you don't mind."

Goodykoontz waved a hand, and Perlmutter performed the chore. When Calhoun had taken his first sip of the smooth but much preferred rye, Goodykoontz said, "I am the supervisor of the Santa Rita Exploring and Mining Company. As such, I am in nominal control of Tubac. The nearest law is in Mesilla, some four hundred miles east of here."

Calhoun nodded, indicating that he knew where Mesilla was.

"I try to run a tidy, peaceful town here, Mr. . . . ." He could not stop from trying to find out the man's name. It worked no better this time than it had before. "Generally, I think I do a pretty good job. Oh, there's always some damned Mexican who gets a snootful of mescal and raises a ruckus of a time, but that's about it."

Calhoun knew for certain Goodykoontz was spouting nonsense, but he saw no need to point that out. "I like a quiet town," Calhoun said blandly.

"Good, good," Goodykoontz said, his flabby face beaming. "And I think we'd both like to keep it that way."

Calhoun shrugged. "I haven't caused any trouble. Ain't plannin' to neither."

"Then what do you call thumping the bejesus out of Reese Tate a little while ago?"

"He that smirkin' little fart with the swole-up head come against me out in the street?"

Goodykoontz could not contain the smile that curled up his tiny mouth. "Yes."

"That, Mr. Goodykoontz, was a lesson in manners."

Goodykoontz smiled again. "Indeed." His opinion of this man rose quite a bit. "But I'd be obliged if you were to not offer such lessons anymore."

"Keep such pests away from me, and I'll not have to swat 'em."

Goodykoontz nodded. "I'd also be obliged if you were to tell me your name. I like knowing who I'm speaking to."

"Wade Calhoun," he said after only a moment's hesitation. He saw no reason not to tell Goodykoontz his name.

"I have occasional need for men like you, Mr. Calhoun," Goodykoontz said thoughtfully. "I think it'd be beneficial to both of us to work together, rather than at cross-purposes."

"I ain't lookin' for a job," he said truthfully. Calhoun figured to spend a few days here relaxing, then hit the trail. It didn't matter to where.

"I can make it worth your while."

"How?" Calhoun had nothing against picking up some extra cash now and again, if all it involved was varmint control.

Goodykoontz spread his plump, lily white hands wide, expansively. "The amenities of the bar would be yours to enjoy. Free, of course. Likewise with the . . . rooms out back."

"Rooms?" Calhoun asked, interest piqued. He had

a thought on what that meant, but wanted to make sure.

"The finest ladies between New Orleans and San Francisco, Mr. Calhoun." Goodykoontz was quite proud of that fact, and was not ashamed to show it.

Calhoun nodded and drained the glass of rye. He held the glass out. Perlmutter refilled it. Calhoun puffed a few moments, then asked, through the cloud of smoke, "And just what am I to do for these amenities?"

"An odd job now and then."

Calhoun thought about it. He was not a man used to finery and comforts. Such living was a rare treat for him, and he preferred it that way, since it would not lose its luster too quickly. He considered accepting the offer, making use of the saloon and the beds of the fallen angels for a day or two and then riding out before payment became due.

He sighed. He was not that kind of a man. He drained the glass of rye and set the glass on the edge of the desk. "I'm obliged for the offer, Mr. Goodykoontz," he said with the barest hint of regret, "but I expect I'll have to turn you down."

"Why?" Goodykoontz asked, surprised.

"I don't like bein' beholden to anybody."

Goodykoontz nodded, but added as Calhoun started to rise, "Wait a minute, please, Mr. Calhoun." When Calhoun had settled his rump into the chair again, Goodykoontz said, "Why don't you partake of things here, free—just for a day or so. You still feel the same then, well"—he shrugged his large, rounded shoulders—"you can go your own way in peace. Won't owe me anything. What say?"

Calhoun figured there was more behind Goodykoontz's offer than a kindly heart. Still, it wouldn't hurt to take advantage of the offer. He figured he could turn his back on Goodykoontz later, and do so with a clear conscience. "Reckon that wouldn't put me out," he offered.

"Good, good." Goodykoontz beamed again. "Well, enjoy yourself." As Calhoun turned and walked out, Goodykoontz nodded his head. He was certain the fine liquors, smooth cigars, excellent food, and talented, pleasing women he had offered Calhoun would soon turn Calhoun's head his way. It was much easier than trying to force a hard case like Wade Calhoun into doing something he was dead set against.

CHAPTER

* 10 *

Calhoun walked into Goodykoontz's saloon, as he called it for want of a better name, and took a seat with his back to one of the thick adobe walls. His placement gave him a commanding view of the entire room, as well as of the door.

A chubby waiter with an off-white shirt, arm garters, and string tie walked over. Calhoun ordered a bottle of rye. As it had been the night before, the whiskey was delivered promptly. It was set, along with a crystal glass, on the table. The waiter disappeared again, without asking for money.

This is the life, Calhoun thought as he poured some of the amber liquid into the glass. He rolled a cigarette, lit it, and then leaned back in his chair. As he sipped and puffed, he thought back over the past twenty hours or so. It had been a little bit of an eventful time.

After leaving Goodykoontz's company, Calhoun had considered stopping at the bar. But he decided he had some other things to do, so he walked straight outside. He had not realized until then how well adobe could insulate against the punishing heat of the Sonoran Desert. The difference was apparent as soon as he walked outside. Not that the saloon and office had been all that cool—unless one compared it with the blast furnace of the outside.

It took Calhoun a little longer to decide not to head out to the back, where the women were set up in smaller adobe buildings. He managed to restrain himself without too much effort, however, and strolled toward Juan Sosa's store.

As he came out at the end of the trail that ran between the vast piles of goods, Calhoun saw that Sosa and one customer were the only ones in the place. Calhoun stepped to the side and folded his arms over his chest, watching without much interest as Sosa attended to his customer—a woman whom Calhoun could not see well, but who appeared at a glance to be out of place here.

The woman apparently had heard him enter. She finished looking at the cloth Sosa held for her, and then she looked at Calhoun. Calhoun nodded in her direction.

The woman was as plain as a Shaker's wood chair. She was tall, and rather slim, but she somehow still seemed substantial, with a pioneer woman's sturdiness.

The woman smiled a little. It seemed tired, as did her plain, unlined face. The shock of long, slightly curly, reddish-brown hair framed her thin face. She gave the impression of being worn down by life, but unyielding to the pressure. Her face was dark from the sun and wind, not from her heritage, and Calhoun wondered what an Anglo woman was doing in Sosa's store.

"I might be a spell, mister," she said in a husky

voice, one much deeper than most women pos-
sessed. "If your business here won't take long, I'll
wait a bit."

"I'm in no hurry, ma'am," Calhoun said, surprising
himself more than a little. All he wanted to do was
speak with Sosa for a few minutes. But there was
something in the woman's stance, in her demeanor,
that made him want to just stand here and watch
her for a while.

The woman nodded curtly and turned back to her
business. There seemed to be no nonsense about
her. She simply knew what had to be done, and she
went ahead and did it.

Calhoun kept an eye on her as she moved about
in the small store. Here, too, she was all business.
She looked at dry goods, felt produce, hefted a bag
of salt. Whenever she spoke, it was with the same
deep, resonant voice. Calhoun found himself
intrigued by her. He found her openness enchanting;
her businesslike attitude refreshing; her strong,
sure movements somewhat enticing. That surprised
him, since she seemed to be formed mostly of long,
lean, sharp planes.

He wondered about her, how she had gotten to
Tubac, why she was shopping in Sosa's.

From the woman's talking with Sosa, Calhoun
learned that her name was Señora Viejo. Calhoun
began to regret not having taken Señora Viejo up on
her offer to get his business over with quickly and be
gone. He had been interested in her, but now that he
had learned she was married, his interest waned. Still,
he had said he would wait, and he would keep his

word. Besides, she was still quite pleasant to watch.

He eventually rolled a cigarette and lit it, puffing away as he leaned against a stack of crates. Shortly after stubbing out the cigarette butt under the toe of his boot on the hard-packed dirt floor, Señora Viejo finished her business. She nodded at Calhoun as she moved smoothly by him and up the track that led out of the store.

Calhoun waited a moment, unmoving, letting a picture of Señora Viejo linger in his mind. He figured it would be the last time he would see her, and he was sort of sorry to see her go, since he had invested twenty minutes or so watching her and enjoyed it.

He sighed and moved forward.

"Gracias, señor," Sosa said after putting down a jug from which he had just taken a long swallow.

"For what?" He reached for the basket-wrapped earthen jug that Sosa was holding out.

"For waiting."

Calhoun shrugged and hauled the jug up to his lips. The rank mescal sizzled hotly down his throat. He pulled the jug away and set it on the counter.

"Most men would not have waited for Señora Viejo to finish." Sosa looked sad.

"I take it she's married to a Mexican?" Calhoun questioned. "She don't look like she's Mexican herself."

"Sí." Sosa shook his head sadly as he pulled the jug closer to him. "Poor Señora Viejo."

Calhoun wondered what that meant. His slightly raised eyebrows asked the question for him.

"Señor Viejo died in the mines almost a year ago. The señora's life has not been easy since then."

"She doesn't seem to be takin' it too hard." Calhoun's interest in the woman was piqued again.

"She is a strong woman, señor," Sosa said. He took another drink, then rolled tobacco in a corn husk. As he lit it, he added, "But a woman can only handle so much trouble."

"She got troubles beyond bein' a widow?"

"*Sí.*" His old brown eyes crinkled up from the smoke wreathing his head. "Not too many men— Anglo men—look favorably on an Anglo woman who has been married to . . ." His voice got a hitch in it. "To one of my people."

"I expect that's true enough," Calhoun said evenly. While it didn't bother him, he knew it would bother a lot of other men. Many of them would treat Señora Viejo as little better than a fallen angel.

"Well, what can I do for you, Señor Calhoun?" Sosa asked as he dropped the *cigarrillo* and stomped it out.

"Not so much anything you can do." He paused and took a drink.

After Calhoun set the jug down, Sosa stuck the cork back in the top and he stored it below. "Then what is it?" The old man looked more than a little worried.

"I had me a chat with Mr. Goodykoontz just a bit ago."

Sosa's worry increased considerably.

"He seems to think I had somethin' to do with Wilson's death. I told him I didn't."

"And?" Sosa's voice quavered.

"He suggested he might come ask you about it."

Sosa felt a coldness sprout in the pit of his stomach.

It spread rapidly, rising faster than a month's growth of good corn. "I told you this would bring trouble, señor," he breathed, voice creaking out of his aging, constricted throat.

Calhoun almost smiled, seeing the fear on Sosa's face. "So I let it be known to him that should you be asked any questions about such a thing, I'd look on it poorly."

The relief was nearly as fast in coming as had the fear. But almost as quickly, it was tempered by a renewal of the fear. Madison Goodykoontz was not a man easily scared or put off. He would not be threatened by anyone, not even a hard man like Wade Calhoun.

"I expect he'll not bother you."

"But you cannot be sure, señor," Sosa said.

"No," Calhoun allowed. "But Goodykoontz'll know it ain't worth him gettin' killed just to ask you if I shot one of his punks."

Sosa stared at Calhoun. Never before had he heard someone speak of Goodykoontz in such a way. He realized, though, that Calhoun made sense. Slade Wilson was a low-level thug on Goodykoontz's staff of gunmen. The mining company chief would not be too put out by Wilson's death.

"You think that's true, señor?" Sosa asked hopefully.

Calhoun nodded. "Should he be fool enough to send somebody over here to bother you, though, you send for me. Understand?"

"*Sí.*" Sosa felt much better now.

Calhoun turned and took two steps. Suddenly he stopped and turned back. "You think Señora Viejo'd object to me callin' on her?"

Sosa grinned and shook his head.

"Where's she live?"

Sosa scratched out a hasty map on a scrap of paper and held it out. Calhoun took it, glanced at it, nodded, and stuck the paper into a shirt pocket. "Obliged, Mr. Sosa," he said before heading out.

Calhoun went back to his room and rested a bit. After a meal of enchiladas and coffee with Señora Alvarez, Calhoun cleaned his weapons. He hadn't used them since killing Wilson, but he was compulsive almost in his wanting to keep them in the best of shape.

Afterward, he walked Señora Alvarez several blocks to the house of a friend. Leaving her there, he strolled through the cooling, dark streets of Tubac. Had it not been dark already, he might have called on Señora Viejo, but he thought that would be improper now.

Instead, he turned his steps toward Goodykoontz's saloon. There he enjoyed a quarter of a bottle of good rye whiskey. Finally he called the waiter over. "How do I make arrangements for a woman?" he asked, unembarrassed.

The waiter was nonplussed at the question. "When you're ready, I'll bring you to Madame Cartouche. After that, it's up to you."

"I expect I can handle it," Calhoun said dryly, hackles rising just a bit.

"Didn't say you couldn't, Mr. Calhoun," the waiter said smoothly. "Just sayin' that's the way it works."

Calhoun finished off the whiskey left in the glass and stood. "Lead on," he said.

* * *

Two hours later he let himself into his room in Señora Alvarez's house. Sated with food, whiskey, and a woman, he had no trouble in getting to sleep. He did not bother to worry—or even think about—what the next day would bring. He might no longer be welcomed at Goodykoontz's saloon and brothel.

He got no trouble though, and was not asked for money when he ordered his whiskey. As he sat there drinking, he knew that this could not last forever. Probably not even another day or two.

Normally, there would be no problem. Indeed, he hadn't planned on staying much longer than this anyway. Now, however, he wasn't so sure. He had a hankering to meet and get to know Señora Viejo. For some reason he saw it as a challenge. He wasn't sure why, though he suspected it was that he hadn't found such a challenge in a long time. Besides, he had paid for a week at Señora Alvarez's.

He sighed and sipped some more before rolling another cigarette. He was not one for worrying about things. He took life as it came. He would enjoy Goodykoontz's hospitality as long as it lasted. Then, and only then, would he decide what to do next.

For now, though, there was good whiskey, plenty of tobacco, Señora Alvarez's excellent cooking, as well as the food at the saloon here, and the women out back. And, he added mentally, there was the little matter of trying to conquer Señora Viejo.

CHAPTER

* 11 *

Señora Viejo proved not all that difficult to conquer. Or at least not as far as meeting her. Calhoun simply walked up to her adobe house and knocked strongly on the door.

Señora Viejo appeared, wiping her long, strong hands on her dingy apron. "Yes?" she asked. There was neither invitation nor rejection in her voice.

"I was wonderin' if you'd mind was I to come a courtin' you, ma'am," Calhoun said quietly.

"You know about me?"

Calhoun scratched his jaw, feeling the growth of several days worth of stubble. "That you was married to a Señor Viejo and that you're now a widow? Yep."

"Then why do you want to come courtin' me for?" Señora Viejo dropped the apron and stood with her hands on her sharp hipbones. She was no beauty, she knew full well, and did not have a heap of men coming to her door to court her. She suspected this one had an ulterior motive.

Calhoun looked at the dim figure in the doorway, noting the sharp chin, the strong angle of her jaw, the worn, plain brown cotton dress covered by the stark gray apron. Her hair had been put up in some fashion, but it was straying considerably now, and she still looked tired or worn.

Calhoun shrugged. "Thought it'd be a pleasurable thing to do, ma'am." He hesitated a heartbeat. "For us both."

"I ain't the kind to lightly call folks a liar, mister, but I ain't given over to keepin' my mouth shut when I got somethin' to say. And I think you're a liar, Mr. . . . ?"

"Wade Calhoun."

"Mr. Calhoun."

Calhoun stared at her. He could see in her face the hard life she had lived, the insults she had suffered because of her marriage to a Mexican man, the toughness of just living in such a desolate place. It was not a place for the faint-hearted, and he knew just by looking at her that she was not a weakling.

"I ain't," he said simply.

It was Señora Viejo's turn to stare. She took in the hard, pocked face, the calm, steady gaze of the deep blue eyes, the lean, powerful lines of his body. *This one ain't like the others,* she thought. *There's a heap more to him.*

"I might believe you, Mr. Calhoun," she said slowly. "Why don't you step inside here? We'll sit and have some coffee."

"Won't folks talk about you, ma'am?"

"My late husband's folks won't. The Anglos'll talk about me no matter what," Señora Viejo said matter-of-factly. She stepped out of the way, leaving him some room.

Calhoun could understand that people would act that way. He was a little puzzled though. "You trust me, ma'am?" he asked.

"Nope," Señora Viejo said flatly. "But I figure if you mean me harm, you'll do it whether I object to it or not. If you are tellin' the truth, I reckon I ought to give you a chance to prove it." She shrugged.

She had been without a man for a year, ever since Jaime had died. A few of the Mexican men—friends of Jaime's for the most part—had offered to marry her, but she needed time to grieve. They understood and left her alone.

She had gotten far more attention, in the form of crude propositions, from more than a few of the Anglo men in Tubac. All but one of those men had been turned away after a little by her disinterest and her cold demeanor. That other one had tried to press his case with force, until she had almost gutted him with a butcher knife. He had thought of getting back at her for it, but quickly realized that to do so, he would have to admit that it was she who had cut him in the first place. He chose, instead, to ride for parts unknown once he had recovered.

Calhoun stepped inside. It was a small place, two dirt-floored rooms—a bedroom at back, hidden from view by a blanket, and this room, which took in the kitchen, eating area, and what in some homes might have been a sitting area.

The house smelled of herbs, spices, wet adobe, dust and decay. It smelled of hard times and pain and neglect. Still, there was something else in the air, the scent of a woman's care. It gave Calhoun an odd feeling, one he had not felt since Kansas, before the Sioux had come. Before Lizbeth and Lottie had died.

"Sit," Señora Viejo said, waving toward the sturdy,

plain table and the matching chairs. She moved toward the stove. She pulled up her apron and used it as a pot holder as she lifted the coffeepot and poured two cups of coffee. She set the pot down and carried the cups to the table. She put one in front of Calhoun and the other by an empty chair. She turned toward her cupboards. In a moment she returned with a plate of cookies.

Calhoun sat at the chair facing the door, and watched her as she worked. He was almost comfortable doing so, which made him distinctly uncomfortable.

"Molasses cookies," Señora Viejo said as she took her seat across from Calhoun. She half smiled. "I loved Jaime very much, Mr. Calhoun," she said in a monotone. "And because of that, I came to love Mexican food. But of a time, I've got to have some of my own things."

"Jaime was your husband?"

Señora Viejo nodded as she bit into one of the cookies.

An uncomfortable silence grew and surrounded the two. Finally, Calhoun asked, "What happened to your husband?" He didn't really care all that much, but he had to say something just to break the silence.

"They told me he was caught in a rock slide at the mine." She had gotten over her grief, but she still did not like to talk about it.

"You don't believe them." It was not really a question.

"No," Señora Viejo said flatly. She hesitated, wondering if she should speak. Then she decided she should. They could not do anything worse to her than had already been done. "I think someone killed him."

"Why?"

Señora Viejo shrugged. She neither knew nor cared. She only knew that it had been done, and that she could do nothing about it.

Calhoun nodded. Once again the quiet descended and covered them. Calhoun rolled a cigarette and lit it. He and Señora Viejo drank their coffee. After he had stomped the cigarette out on the floor, Calhoun rose. "It's been a pleasure, ma'am," he said. He looked at her but could read nothing on her face.

She rose and escorted him to the door. As Calhoun stepped outside, he turned. "You mind if I come callin' again, ma'am?"

"No," she answered. "No, I wouldn't." She surprised herself a little with the ease she had said the words. She had decided somewhere in the past, discomfiting hour that Wade Calhoun could be trusted. It had been nothing he had said or done; the decision had just come to her.

He had disappeared around the corner of a house down the way. Señora Viejo realized she had been watching him. She turned and headed back to the table to clean up the few small dishes.

Two days later Señora Viejo told Calhoun her maiden name—Lucille Ostergaard. They grew more comfortable together, and Calhoun began squiring Lucille around town. She was a little reluctant at first to be seen around Tubac, especially in the company of a man, but she quickly got used to it.

Indeed, though their relationship still consisted

of great gobs of silence, she swiftly blossomed under its spell. Her face was brighter and she walked with a firmer step. She was no fool, and knew that Calhoun could be using her, but she began to think that was doubtful.

The only sticky part was knowing that people were talking about them. None of them would do it in public that she could tell, and she assumed that was because of Calhoun. He was a hard man with a hard look about him. And after the thrashing he had given to Reese Tate, not too many men were willing to go against him. Still, she heard the whispers, and they hurt her like they always did, though she never let on.

Lucille was worried, however, that the whispers would grow in intensity, until Calhoun heard them. Then, she figured, blood would be shed. She was deathly afraid for Calhoun, having come to love him far more than she knew was good for her. She had lost one man; she did not think she could handle losing another.

Her only other worry was that he did not care for her. She was certain after a few days that he was not using her. She was as equally certain that he did not love her. But she hoped beyond hope that he at least liked her more than a little. If she found out that he hardly cared for her at all, that would be as devastating as losing him to violence.

A week after Calhoun had first come to her door, Lucille invited him over for supper. He walked toward Lucille's place from Señora Alvarez's in the growing darkness. Despite the fact that the sun had gone down, it was still hotter than the back side of hell. He arrived and knocked.

Lucille answered the door, looking self-conscious. She felt that way because she had put on her only good dress—dark blue calico with white lace trim. It covered from neck to ankle; and the sleeves went to the wrist. A silver brooch was pinned to the left side of the buttoned bodice. The garment softened a little the hard plainness of Lucille's face.

Calhoun hid his surprise as he hung his hat on a peg next to the door and then took his seat.

Lucille hid her discomfort by bustling about the kitchen area and serving up food. Then she finally sat. "Dig in," she said quietly, beginning to think she had made a fool of herself with all this fuss.

Calhoun looked at her simple, open face for a moment. He was attracted to her entirely too much, he knew. It was not a good feeling, and he resolved to move out of Tubac soon, putting Lucille Viejo, and Tubac, behind him.

For now, though, there was what appeared to be a sumptuous meal waiting. He heaped his plate full of baked chicken, potatoes, beans and biscuits and began eating. He liked Mexican food, he had found, but after more than a week of nothing else, he was grateful for the fare he was more used to.

Afterward, they sipped coffee, and Calhoun smoked a cigarette. Calhoun was still rather amazed at how little either felt the need to speak. It was a relief to him to not have to think he had to be jabbering all the time. He was a man sparing of speech in general, and to have to make small talk with a woman, even one he was courting, was not his way. He was glad he did not have to play that game.

He had a snort of whiskey and another hand-rolled cigarette while Lucille cleared away the dinner mess.

When she finished that, she turned and walked straight to him. She had decided to do this two days ago, and had had second thoughts ever since. Now, though, was not the time for that. She had made up her mind, and she would proceed.

Lucille held out her hands. Calhoun looked up at her in surprise and took them in his own hard, callused paws. Lucille tugged a little, and Calhoun rose effortlessly. Holding one of Calhoun's hands, Lucille led him toward the back room.

"This ain't necessary, Luce, you know," he said as she stopped alongside the bed and turned to face him. She was nearly as tall as Calhoun was, and undaunted by him.

"Maybe so, maybe not," she said, looking him square in the eyes. Now that she had made the move, her nervousness had vanished. "But I'm goin' ahead with it." She paused and let a slight smile crawl over her thin lips. "Unless you ain't willin'."

He wrapped his arms around her and kissed her hard. If was some time before he pulled away. "I seem willin' enough to suit you, ma'am?" he asked in a growl.

"Yessir," Lucille breathed. She hadn't felt like this in years. Not since the first time Jaime and she had been together as man and wife. That had been her first time, and there had been no other man since. Only Jaime. Until now.

Calhoun began undoing the buttons of Lucille's bodice. She clutched at him.

* * *

It was almost dawn when Calhoun left Lucille's, after a filling breakfast of eggs, *chorizo,* and coffee. Neither had gotten much sleep. When Calhoun got back to Señora Alvarez's, he crawled into bed and fell asleep, tired but happy. And more than a little perplexed over his feelings for Lucille Viejo.

CHAPTER

* 12 *

Despite the fact that nearly a week and a half had passed, Calhoun's free ride at Goodykoontz's saloon had not stopped. He was surprised at that, but he figured that Goodykoontz was still trying to interest him in becoming one of his hired guns. Calhoun supposed that the rotund mining supervisor figured that by letting Calhoun continue to come into the saloon and have everything free, that eventually Calhoun would be beholden to him.

It might also be, Calhoun thought, that Goodykoontz assumed that since Calhoun was still coming to the saloon so frequently that he had already made an unwritten contract to work for Goodykoontz. Calhoun almost smiled at thinking how disappointed Goodykoontz would be when he realized that Calhoun had no intention of ever working for him.

Calhoun had taken to going to the saloon every afternoon for a spell, sipping good whiskey and puffing on fine cigars. Then he would usually take a nap—he had learned long ago to sleep whenever the opportunity presented itself, since there were plenty of times he had to do without. As darkness began to fall, he would go over to Lucille's for dinner. The past several days, he had also been spending the night.

Señora Alvarez was a little disappointed in his more frequent absences, but she understood. She knew that a young, strong man like Wade Calhoun would need a young woman, not a worn-out old thing like her. Still, she missed seeing him as often as she had earlier, though she resigned herself to having a late breakfast or early lunch with him each day.

She could not forget, either, that the money he paid for the room was welcome.

Calhoun knew how the plump old woman felt, but there was nothing he could, or would, do for her. There were times when he was almost sorry that he had gotten mixed up at all with Lucille Viejo, and so he didn't need the complications of trying to be overly friendly with Señora Alvarez, too.

Three days after he had spent his first night with Lucille, Calhoun entered Goodykoontz's saloon as usual. These days he didn't even have to order. The waiter just appeared with a bottle, a glass, and a small silver platter on which sat three medium-sized cigars and a box of lucifers.

Calhoun nodded, bit the end off a cigar, and lit it. Holding the cigar in his teeth, he eased the cork out of the bottle and then filled the glass. After his first shot, he looked around the room.

The usual assortment of gunmen and small-time officials of one kind or another were there, though there seemed to be more of them than was common, and Calhoun noted that several of them seemed to be newcomers. At least he hadn't seen them. Of course, that didn't mean anything. Tubac might be a small town by St. Louis standards, but Calhoun figured it was the biggest city between Mesilla and the West Coast. As such, it would attract travelers, government officials, mining executives, vagabonds, and anyone within a thousand miles who held to the hope of finding riches in the bowels of the earth.

Three of the men he had never seen appeared to be watching him. He ignored them for the most part, other than to make sure they weren't about to try something. They left an hour later, and Calhoun went back to his solitary drinking.

The three were out in the street, leaning against the building next to Goodykoontz's saloon, when Calhoun headed outside into the vision-shattering brilliance of the sun. The three men stepped forward, almost as if pulled by a single rope.

"Hey, mister," one of them said loudly. "Just hold on there a minute."

Calhoun stopped and faced the three men. As he made the slight turn, he slid the small loop off the hammer of both Dragoons. He was wary but prepared to listen— if they had anything to really say. After all, many was the time he had been hired on for jobs by men who looked a lot worse than this crew. These three were fairly well dressed, in clean wool pants, almost-new cotton or butternut shirts, good though dusty boots, and high-crowned hats. Two had bandannas around their necks.

The one who had spoken wore a lone Colt revolver at his right side, high up. He moved up fairly close to Calhoun. The other two hung back a little and flanked the first man. One of those wore a Remington in a cross-draw holster. The third had two Colts, one riding on each hip.

"Well?" Calhoun finally said. He was rather impatient. He had gotten used to a siesta in the hottest part of the day, and looked forward to it. He did not like the idea of standing out here in the broiling heat waiting for someone to think of what he had to say.

The man smirked a little. "Well, me and my friends here was wonderin' how much you'd take to let us spend an hour or so with the woman."

Calhoun managed to control his temper, but barely. He spun and began walking away.

"Hey, goddammit," the same man yelled. "Wait a minute. Come on back here and talk with us some. We got us a proposition to make you." He paused, but Calhoun had not stopped. "We figure that if that trollop of yours was bein' poked by a bean-eatin' goddamn Mexican all them years, and now she's takin' you on, she ought to be willin' to have a go with us three. We figured you wouldn't mind pickin' up some extra cash. Hell, that's what pimps do, dammit."

Calhoun whirled, a Dragoon in hand. Without hesitation, he fired twice. Both balls punctured the talker's heart. A quarter dollar could have covered both holes in his chest.

Calhoun swung little to his right, toward the nearest of the other two men. He fired twice more, cutting him down.

The third man twirled and ran. Calhoun fired the last ball in the Dragoon. The bullet took the fleeing man in the back of the leg, halfway between knee and buttock. He jerked forward as the shattered leg no longer worked properly. He scrambled forward, dragging his leg behind, still trying frantically to get away, to find some sort of shelter.

Calhoun calmly dropped the Dragoon into his holster and pulled the other. He walked toward the struggling man. The man heard him coming, and glanced fearfully back over his shoulder several times.

As Calhoun neared, the man suddenly stopped his frantic crawl. He flopped over, trying to ignore the pain in his leg, and reached with his right hand for the Remington in the cross-draw holster.

Calhoun fired, putting a ball through the man's right shoulder. The Remington fell in the dirt. Calhoun walked up to the man and placed a foot on his chest, flattening the man down in the dust. He cocked the Dragoon and aimed it at the man's head.

"Who put you up to this, boy?" Calhoun asked, voice harsh.

"Nobody," the man answered, wide-eyed and sweating. Pain coursed through his body, and he expected death at any moment.

"This your idea?"

"No, no," the man babbled. "It was all Sparks's idea."

"Who's he?"

"The one you . . ." The man hesitated. "The one who did all the talkin' before."

"And what was the idea of such a damn fool stunt?" Calhoun was certain there was more to this than the bleeding man was letting on.

"Nothin', mister. Jesus, we just wanted to rile you a little. Hell," he added defensively, "you got to expect that when you court a . . . a . . . hell, a white woman who was married to a Mex."

"I do?" Calhoun recoiled at the very sight of this man, and the sour memory of the past few minutes.

"Well, hell, there's somethin' wrong about such things. Jesus, it ain't right that a white woman should go off and lay with a greas . . . with a Mexican. Damn, that's near about as bad as if he was an Injun."

"And so Sparks just up and decided to bust my ass about it?" Calhoun asked, growling. None of it made any sense, but he was sure he wasn't going to get anything more out of this man. He was also pretty sure that this man knew nothing about it. He had simply followed the man named Sparks.

"Yeah, yeah." Lester Miles was still worried, but he thought that maybe since he really didn't know anything, this maniac would leave him be. "We just figured that maybe you'd be open to . . . well, you know . . . lettin' us have a crack at her."

Calhoun suddenly realized that this man was an idiot, an oaf who was easy to dupe. His friends had gotten his mind onto the possible chance of a lustful fling with a woman he saw as completely wanton. With that, they had gone about their business for their own purposes, while this one plodded along in their shadow.

Calhoun sighed. He hated to shoot such a fool, but he had no real choice. "Stupid son of a bitch," he muttered. Then he pulled the trigger.

With the Dragoon still in hand, just in case, Calhoun turned and walked away. No one bothered him, but he was almost to Señora Alvarez's house before he slid the gun away. He entered the house and saw Señora Alvarez in the kitchen.

"I'll be pullin' out, ma'am," he said quietly. He had

made up his mind on the way over here. He didn't really think anyone would come looking for him to pay for the shootings of the three men, but one could never be sure in a place like Tubac. He didn't want to jeopardize the few people he had come to know and like in the town, like Señora Alvarez and Lucille.

Señora Alvarez looked stricken. "When?" she asked. She would miss having this hard-bitten young man around, though his company had been rather infrequent of late. She would also miss his money.

"Soon's I get my things together."

"Oh, no," Señora Alvarez whispered. "But you have paid for another week."

"Keep the money, ma'am." He knew she could use it far more than he could.

"Are you in trouble, Señor Calhoun?" she asked.

He shrugged. "Might be. If it comes, though, I don't want you gettin' involved in it."

"Where will you go?"

Calhoun shook his head. "Head to Tucson, I reckon. From there . . ." He shrugged again. He had no real intention of doing any such a thing. It could be seen as running away, and the very thought of that made him almost ill. Besides, he still had his feelings about Lucille Viejo to work out, which could take a little time.

"But . . ."

"I've got no time for chattin', señora," Calhoun said politely. He headed out of the room before she could argue. It did not take him long to pack, since he had little.

Once outside, he wondered where he should go. He had no horse, and might have trouble getting one, if he was being sought. Also, if anyone was looking for him, they most likely would go to Lucille's or here, and then the other. He needed to get in contact with Lucille, though, not only to explain what had happened, but also to try to get some help in buying a horse.

Once he did that, he could ride out of town but stay nearby to see if what passed for the law around here came for him. If so, he would decide how to deal with it when it happened. If not, he could just return in a few days, if he thought that proper. Still, he needed a place to lay low for the rest of the afternoon, and overnight.

He stepped off, deciding he needed to see Lucille first. He would explain to her, and see if she knew of someone who could help him. He strolled boldly down the streets, unafraid of anyone. It was almost as if he dared someone to try to cause trouble.

Besides, he couldn't very well flit from shadow to shadow when he was lugging the expensive, fancy saddle, with the two heavy Walker pistols, the Henry rifle and Greener shotgun, his saddlebags and bedroll.

As he neared Lucille's house, however, he slowed and moved more cautiously. His eyes flicked from side to side, trying to take in everything. All seemed in order.

Calhoun opened the wood door to the small adobe storage shed alongside the house. He dropped his gear off and then headed for the house. As he reached for the door handle, he called out, "Luce, I'm comin' in." It still gave him a strange feeling. It was as if he were married again, or maybe still.

He stepped inside.

CHAPTER

✳ 13 ✳

Calhoun's right hand darted for one of the Dragoons, but he stopped immediately, frozen, when he heard a quiet, firm "Don't." The fact that a cocked pistol was pressed lightly against each side of his head made a difference, too.

Probably the main reason that he froze, though, was the sight of Lucille being held in a chair by two men. Each man had one hard hand on her shoulder, and were aiming a revolver at her with the other. Through the house's dimness, he could see that she looked mostly calm. Maybe a little worried, but certainly not frightened.

Lucille was frightened, though she was striving not to show it. She wasn't concerned for herself, but for Calhoun. She was worried that his hot temper would get the better of him, and he would try to do something to save her, getting himself killed in the process. She didn't much care about herself, and whether she died or not. But she would be devastated if he was to be killed here.

She was a little relieved when Calhoun slowly raised both hands, not wanting to make any sudden moves that might startle any of the gunmen. He waited patiently as another man pulled the two Dragoons out of the holsters, removed the big Bowie knife from around his shoulder, and took the pointed dagger out of the sheath on the pistol belt. He made no reaction when he realized that the man had missed the backup weapon he carried under his shirt at the small of his back.

Harry Perlmutter stepped out of the shadows. "Afternoon, Mr. Calhoun," he said calmly.

Calhoun did not respond.

"Mr. Goodykoontz would like to see you." Still no response from Calhoun. "I expect you to come along with us like a good fellow." He paused momentarily. "And, please, no trouble, either here or while you're with Mr. Goodykoontz, eh. Blackie and Four Eyes will be stayin' here with Señora Viejo to make sure you behave. That understood?"

Calhoun nodded once. He turned his gaze from Perlmutter to the two men holding Lucille in the chair. "I presume," he said with deadly menace, "that Señora Viejo will be unmolested."

"She will," Perlmutter vowed. He did not look at his two cronies. His word carried the weight of Madison Goodykoontz behind it. They would obey—or suffer the consequences. "As long as you give us no trouble." Just in case Calhoun was unclear on the matter, Perlmutter added, "The first sign of trouble from you, and I'll turn Blackie and Four Eyes loose."

Calhoun nodded, understanding. "Let's go, then," he said.

Perlmutter nodded, and the guns suddenly were no longer pointed at Calhoun's head. Calhoun knew, however, that they were still in the men's hands, and that he could not try anything. "Lead the way, Mr. Calhoun," Perlmutter said, the faintest hint of a smile on his face.

Calhoun turned and walked out the door, knowing he had at least two guns pointing at his back. The two who had pointed pistols were back there, as was the man who had relieved him of his weapons.

"What's Mr. Goodykoontz want to see me about, Mr. Perlmutter?" he asked over his shoulder as they walked down the street.

"Mr. Goodykoontz will answer that," Perlmutter said with finality.

It did not take long to make the short walk to Goodykoontz's saloon, through it under the interested gaze of the patrons, and then into the quiet, almost cool back room from which Madison Goodykoontz ruled.

"Sit," Perlmutter said firmly.

Calhoun plopped into one of the stuffed chairs, and shifted so that the small of his back was sort of free. He didn't know as if he might have to try something desperate here, though he was well aware that at least three men were watching him intently, and without a doubt had their pistols trained on him. Perlmutter was leaning against a wall on his left shoulder, just within the periphery of Calhoun's vision.

"I am most disappointed in you, Mr. Calhoun," Goodykoontz said in that high-pitched voice of his. "Most disappointed."

Calhoun shrugged. To him it seemed as if Goodykoontz had never moved from the last time he was here. He wore the same suit, or an exact duplicate, and he sat in the same position, his puffy, ghostly white hands resting across the wide expanse of vest on his belly, fingers laced. The same cloud of odorous lime water hung in the air.

"You have spent a week and a half indulging yourself of my liquors and cigars. Women, too, I suppose." Goodykoontz sighed. "And what do I get in return for my good heart and free hand?" he asked rhetorically. "Three of my employees dead, shot down in the street for no good reason. I told you before I wanted no more trouble in Tubac."

Calhoun shrugged again. "And I told you there wouldn't be any if I was left alone," he said pointedly.

"Having you gun down employees of mine is not exactly what I had in mind when I offered to bring you into my employ, sir."

"I never agreed to join your employ, if you'll recall."

"True." Goodykoontz nodded in agreement. "But since you were partaking of the fruits of my generosity, one would think that you would at least refrain from shooting down men who were in my employ."

"Then you should employ fewer idiots," Calhoun said blandly.

"They were good men, Mr. Calhoun," Goodykoontz said. "Perhaps not the brightest, but good men with a gun, and loyal."

"They were loudmouths and buffoons," Calhoun said evenly.

Goodykoontz nodded. "One hires who one can get," he said in resignation. It was, he had thought more than once, one of the most difficult aspects of a difficult job. There was not enough competent help.

"Look at it this way, Mr. Goodykoontz," Calhoun said dryly. "Now you have some openings, and you can look for folks that ain't such damn fools."

"Indeed," Goodykoontz answered in kind. He paused. "Just what great insult did Sparks, Miles, and Corday heap on you to bring about such a murderous rage?" he asked. He was truly interested in knowing. Having such knowledge might somehow come in handy.

"Wasn't me they insulted, Mr. Goodykoontz."

"Oh?" His glance flicked to Perlmutter, and then back to Calhoun.

"I don't take kindly to sons of bitches insultin' women. Any women. Especially ones I've come to like a bit."

"Ah, the Viejo woman." Goodykoontz nodded in understanding. The look on his face was quite disapproving of the alliance, though he did not voice it. He sighed again. "It's a pity," he said almost dreamily. "Three men—good employees of the Santa Rita Mining and Exploring Company, no less—dead, and all because of a few offhand insults to a woman who . . ." He cut it off, as if coming back to reality.

Calhoun said nothing. He knew that Goodykoontz knew the insults were not offhand, that while the words might not have been thought out beforehand, the course of action had. Those three men had set out to goad Calhoun into something. They had just not foreseen that he could best the three of them in a gunfight. Calhoun more than half suspected that Goodykoontz was behind the whole thing.

"Well, sir," Goodykoontz said with a display of regret he did not feel, "I'm afraid I have no choice." He actually moved then, leaning forward just a little and resting his flabby hands palm down on the desktop. "Since I am the closest thing to the law in these parts, Mr. Calhoun, I'm afraid I'll have to hold you over for a trial in the murders of Sparks, Miles, and Corday."

"Don't seem right to me," Calhoun said evenly. "They were pushin' for a fight, and they got it. They just picked on the wrong man this time."

"You'll have full opportunity to explain your side of it during the trial, Mr. Calhoun," Goodykoontz said reprovingly. "We will hold it three days hence," he added with a firm nod.

Calhoun was less than impressed, and stared blandly at Goodykoontz.

The fat man was annoyed at Calhoun's insolence and lack of regret at what had transpired. He did not show it, though. "You'll be locked up till then, Mr. Calhoun. And I expect you to remain cooperative. Mrs. Viejo will be watched to ensure your cooperation."

Calhoun nodded, then fixed a hard stare on Goodykoontz. "You just best make sure she ain't bothered," he said harshly.

"Is that a threat, Mr. Calhoun?" Goodykoontz asked in a condescending tone.

"Yes," Calhoun told him flatly.

Goodykoontz realized that Calhoun meant it, and knew that somehow Calhoun would make good on the threat. Well, he decided, the threat would only last a few days. Soon after Calhoun's trial would be the hanging. Then the threat would cease, and he could let his men have the trollop for their pleasure, if they could find any in that tall, square-shouldered, plain-faced woman. He nodded. Then he turned his great bulbous head. "Take him to the jail, Mr. Perlmutter."

Calhoun needed no prompting. He simply stood and headed for the door. Perlmutter and the other three men, pistols still out, fell into step behind. Outside the salon Calhoun stopped. "Which way?" he asked.

Following Perlmutter's directions, Calhoun soon found himself in front of a small adobe building down an alleyway toward the river. Two massive mesquite trees shaded it, one from each side. Perlmutter unlocked the door and kicked it open. One of the other men shoved Calhoun lightly on the back. Calhoun entered the dark interior.

The jail house was basically one big room. In the front portion was a desk, a small potbelly stove—more for coffee than for heat, Calhoun figured—and a rack with several rifles and shotguns. About halfway across the room ran iron bars with two doors, and another set of bars divided that into two cells. Both were unoccupied, and contained only a hard iron cot bolted to the outside wall. A small, horizontal window, maybe three feet long and six inches high, ran across the center near the top of the back wall.

The place was musty and crawling with scorpions, black widows, tarantulas, and other assorted insects. They heard an ominous rattle, and one of the men spun and fired three times. The gunfire left a wriggling mass of diamondback rattlesnakes in one corner.

Perlmutter unlocked one of the cell doors and

opened it. "Your gun belt, Mr. Calhoun," he said, holding out his hand.

Calhoun shrugged and removed it. The only thing of any use on it now was his hard-leather pouch, which contained two extra loaded cylinders for the Dragoons, plus a small tin of caps and a dozen or so paper cartridges. Used right, there was enough powder in the pouch to blow the lock off the cell door. Calhoun did not blame Perlmutter for making him remove it.

"Enjoy your stay, Mr. Calhoun," Perlmutter said as Calhoun entered the cell. Perlmutter locked the barred door.

All four men left, Perlmutter locking the wood door behind him, and Calhoun was alone. He sat on the cot and rolled a cigarette, flicking the still burning match at a scorpion. He began taking stock of his situation.

Calhoun had been in worse fixes before, so this held no surprise or concern for him. Changing his outlook, though, were his feelings for Lucille Viejo. He certainly did not love her. That was out of the question. But he had to admit, if only to himself, that he was far more fond of her than he should be. More fond of her than he had been about any woman since Lizbeth. He regretted that now, but there was little he could do to change it.

Because he did care for Lucille, he had to be careful about what he did. Ordinarily, he would've waited until the first time someone brought food, and blast the deliverer as soon as the barred door was open. Then he'd haul out of here. Knowing that Lucille was in danger, though, altered his usual impetuousness.

He decided he would wait to see what happened at the trial. He fully expected to be sentenced to hang. He had received that sentence before, and the hangman hadn't gotten him yet. He was arrogant enough to believe he could cheat the hangman this time, too. There was no telling what opportunities might present themselves to him during the trial. And if they sentenced him to hang, he most likely would have a day or two—probably no more, though—before they carried it out. Goodykoontz seemed the type to want to at least pretend to have legal niceties. Besides, he would need time to make sure all the invited guests to the necktie party arrived.

Calhoun would wait until things looked their bleakest before making some kind of move. He would have some options there, too. He had the backup Walker, and he had a folding knife in his pocket. He could either blast his way out, if that seemed the wisest course, or perhaps use his knife to dig out. These old adobe walls could be breached without much trouble by applying some elbow grease and determination.

Having made that decision, Calhoun rose and walked around the small, dim room, stomping on spiders and other nasty critters. Once he had finished his cigarette and his pest control, he stretched out on the cot, pulled his slouch hat down over his eyes, and faded into sleep.

CHAPTER

* 14 *

Calhoun wondered what the hell all the commotion was about. He could see nothing, but he could hear gunfire, shouts, screams. It all went on for a little more than a half-hour, as best as he could figure.

Silence eventually came. Or at least what seemed silent after all the noise of before. There were still some shouts and neighing horses. Calhoun thought, too, that he could hear—and smell—flames licking at a building.

Calhoun had been in the cell almost two days now. His trial was to be held tomorrow. He had managed to see Lucille twice, under the leering, watchful eyes of Blackie, Four Eyes, and Will Nighswander, the man who had relieved him of his weapons at Lucille's house when he was arrested.

The only other time he saw anyone was twice a day when he was brought food. He didn't know how Señora Alvarez had managed to convince Goodykoontz, or maybe Perlmutter, that she should be the one to provide the provender, but she had. She had kept him filled, too, with large portions of everything.

The first time she had uncovered the tray she was carrying, unveiling the large meal, Four Eyes's eyes widened. "Hell and damnation, but I ain't gonna let you give all that to a man just settin' 'round waitin' for his hangin'.'" He shoved his gold-rimmed spectacles up his nose and reached out to grab a couple of the tamales on the platter.

Calhoun tensed, hand inching around behind him, ready to grab the backup gun. He didn't care about the food so much. It was just that judging by the look in Señora Alvarez's eyes, he might have to kill Blackie and Four Eyes just to stop them from hurting Señora Alvarez.

The old woman suddenly got between the tray, which was sitting on Calhoun's bunk, and Four Eyes. Somehow she managed to scoop up the fork from the tray and plunge it into Four Eyes's forearm.

Four Eyes howled and jerked his arm back. "Damn old whore bitch," he muttered. He drew his right hand back up over his left shoulder to backhand her.

Calhoun shoved the back of his shirt aside and his fingers closed on the wood butt of the cut-down Walker. He was all set to yank it out and send Four Eyes across the divide, but he held himself in check.

"Clyde!" Emmet Blackiston shouted, stopping Calhoun and unknowingly keeping both Four Eyes and himself from getting killed.

Four Eyes cranked his neck around and glared through his glasses at Blackie.

"Mr. Goodykoontz would not be pleased was you to hit that old woman," Blackie said reasonably.

"Hell, she's just some damned old Mexican bitch is all," Four Eyes almost whined. "Mr. Goodykoontz don't like greasers and won't mind."

"He said to see that this old lady brings that murderous son of a bitch his dinner. He didn't say nothin' about knockin' shit out of her. You get fed well enough by Mr. Goodykoontz that you don't need to go grabbin' a dyin' man's nearly last meal." Blackie shook his head. "Hell, I don't know where you put it anyway. Jesus."

Clyde Gates was not tall, and was as thin as Goodykoontz was fat. He looked pretty close to a skeleton dressed in a man's clothes. Blackie had seen his spectacle-wearing friend put away amounts of food that would have fed half a dozen, though.

Four Eyes scowled at Calhoun, who grinned insolently at him, and then at Señora Alvarez. The woman stood there, fork still in hand, threatening.

"Move your fat ass, woman," Four Eyes barked. "Just give the son of a bitch the fork and then get the hell out."

They had left, and Four Eyes caused no more trouble in any of his return visits.

Sitting here now, though, Calhoun wondered what had gone on outside, and wished he could see out. It had sounded like a war going on out there, and he half suspected a band of Apaches had raided Tubac. That was the only thing he could think of that would cause such a commotion.

He learned nothing about it that day. Several hours later than usual, Four Eyes, Blackie, and Señora Alvarez arrived with his supper. As Señora Alvarez placed his supper on the cot, Calhoun asked, "What happened out there today, ma'am?"

"A band of . . ."

"Shut up, old woman," Four Eyes snapped. He looked at Calhoun. "It ain't none of your concern what happened. Your ass ain't long for this world, boy, so nothin' that happens out there should concern you."

Your days are numbered, too, you dumb son of a bitch, Calhoun thought, looking at Four Eyes. He vowed that when the time came to extricate himself from this mess, Four Eyes would be one of the first to die.

Four Eyes jerked his head at Señora Alvarez, indicating she should leave. The woman did. Four Eyes glared at Calhoun a moment. The prisoner looked back evenly, but there was a glint in his eyes that foretold Four Eyes of his death. Four Eyes spun and left, locking the grilled door.

Calhoun put the to-do out of his mind after eating. He smoked a cigarette and decided that whatever had happened had little, if any, effect on him. His main concern right now would be in seeing what happened at his trial tomorrow.

He nodded off earlier than usual, since he wanted to be well rested for the trial. Not that he cared about the trial itself. He was certain his fate had been determined already. He was fairly certain, though, that he would have to make his move then, or shortly after the farcical rite was over.

He was awake and waiting when Four Eyes, Blackie, Nighswander, and Perlmutter came for him. "No breakfast?" he asked dryly.

"You don't need no goddamn breakfast where you're goin', you son of a bitch," Four Eyes growled.

"And there's no need to talk to our guest in such a way," Perlmutter said quietly. "My apologies, Mr. Calhoun."

Calhoun didn't much believe that the apology was sincere, but he nodded in acknowledgment. Perlmutter didn't have to make the effort, of course, and in doing so had shown himself to be a better man than most of the others Calhoun had had to deal with of late.

"Get up," Four Eyes snapped.

To Calhoun, the scrawny little man seemed to be in a constant state of irritation. Calhoun might've been seen as the same way by many people, but he did not make a point of showing it to the whole world all the time. He shook his head as he rose.

"You remember our agreement, don't you, Mr. Calhoun?" Perlmutter asked. "About not causin' trouble."

Calhoun nodded. Even though Blackie and Four Eyes were here, Goodykoontz had plenty of other men at his command. Calhoun was sure Lucille was still being watched over.

"Let's proceed then," Perlmutter said. "Mr. Goodykoontz and the others are waiting."

Calhoun took a look around as they walked. Two buildings were smoldering hulks, and several others showed signs of scorching. They were the only evident signs that something had gone amiss yesterday.

The trial was to be held outside, so that the entire town could attend. A ramada had been constructed in front of Goodykoontz's saloon. Four gnarled mesquite posts served as supports; the top was of interlaced ocotillo. Its shade did little to alleviate the day's already oppressive heat.

Under the ramada was a low-slung wagon, of the kind used by the mines for hauling equipment and men. On the wagon was a table, behind which sat the rotund Madison Goodykoontz. Behind and a little to the left of Goodykoontz's wagon was a matching one. The jury—a dozen men hand-picked by Goodykoontz—sat on it.

Perlmutter and the three other men worked through the crowd and stopped in front of Goodykoontz's wagon. Leaving Blackie, Nighswander, and Four Eyes to watch Calhoun, Perlmutter climbed onto Goodykoontz's wagon and stood to the fat man's right.

When it was quiet in Tubac, except for the sounds of the wind, and birds, and horses, Goodykoontz said, "Mr. Wade Calhoun, you have been charged with the wanton murder of the men known in these parts as Sparks, Miles, and Corday. You have anything to say about it?"

"The damn fools come gunnin' for me and paid the price for it." Calhoun knew it would do him no good, but he was arrogant enough to want people to know that he had taken down three gunmen by himself.

"How did they come gunning for you, sir?" Goodykoontz asked.

Calhoun shrugged.

"I told you that you would have your chance to tell your side of things, Mr. Calhoun," Goodykoontz said with a note of reproof in his voice. "This is your chance, sir. Speak your piece now, or meet the hangman with the knowledge that you did not defend yourself."

Calhoun hated such a farce; hated Goodykoontz making himself out to be some great and benevolent ruler. Calhoun knew damn well that Goodykoontz had already decided his fate, and he was not fond of putting on a show for the residents of Tubac or to display Goodykoontz's "fairness."

On the other hand, Calhoun figured that he should be heard. He knew it would not influence the outcome, but there might be a few people in Tubac who would believe him. They should know not only that he wasn't guilty of cold-blooded murder, but also, Calhoun thought, it might show the townsfolk what kind of man ruled their lives.

"Well?" Goodykoontz encouraged.

"They were insultin' a woman. I took exception to it."

"And who was this woman?"

"Don't matter none."

"I think it does, sir. If she is a fallen woman or something, well, your actions might be seen as, shall we say, misplaced."

Calhoun's temper flared, but he kept it under control. He knew the game Goodykoontz was playing. Goodykoontz wanted it known throughout Tubac that the woman who had brought about the gunplay was in his eyes not a proper, respectable woman. Calhoun figured that Goodykoontz would then have an excuse to find him guilty. It would absolve him of any responsibility of taking on such a burden as pronouncing a death penalty. But Calhoun was not about to play the game for Goodykoontz's benefit.

"She's a widow woman and a . . . friend. But the outcome with those damn fools would've been the same even if I didn't know who she was."

"Come, come, Mr. Calhoun," Goodykoontz said in chiding tones, which he thought imparted reasonableness. "We must know who she is, sir. Again, if she is a Cyprian, there can be no excuse for your murderous assault. However"—the porcine, round shoulders went up and down once—"if she is a respectable, God-

fearing woman, well, that might be considered a miti-
gating circumstance. It could lessen your penalty."

"You know goddamn well who it was," Calhoun said
evenly. "And we both know you've made up your mind
what my fate'll be. I ain't aimin' to stand here and
bandy words with you to make your fat ass look good."

Goodykoontz's face clouded over darkly. He was
angry at Calhoun, but he was more angry at himself.
He should have known Calhoun was no fool; should
have seen that Calhoun could not be bent to his will.
Wade Calhoun was a man who was unafraid of
dying, Goodykoontz realized. He also had the sudden
thought that Calhoun probably looked forward to
the peace of death, to relieve him of whatever
ghosts haunted him.

"Then there is no need for delay," Goodykoontz
said. His voice betrayed none of the anger that
showed on his face. "Gentlemen," he asked over his
shoulder, "what is your decision?"

There was no hesitation. "We find him guilty,"
one man said, speaking for the jury as a whole.

Goodykoontz nodded. He looked at Calhoun,
ready to show the defendant some regret or apology.
He did not, though, realizing suddenly that it would
be misplaced. Calhoun would neither want nor ask
for sympathy. Secretly, Goodykoontz admired that
in Calhoun. "Do you have anything to say before I
pronounce sentence, Mr. Calhoun?" he asked.

Calhoun looked up from where he was rolling a
cigarette. "Nope." He went back to his task. He knew
what was coming, and his mind was half on getting
away from here. The best time, he figured, was the

next time they brought him a meal—unless he was sentenced to hang immediately. Then he would grab the Walker and go out blazing.

He lit the cigarette and looked up at Goodykoontz, sitting in ponderous glory on the wagon.

CHAPTER

∗ 15 ∗

"Mr. Calhoun, I sentence you to hang by the neck until you are dead," Goodykoontz said solemnly.

Calhoun blew out a stream of smoke. All he waited for now was the time of his execution.

"The said sentence will take place in two days' time."

Calhoun was relieved. He would have two days and two nights to pull off his escape. That should be more than enough time. His relief turned to genuine surprise bordering on shock, which he managed to mask, at Goodykoontz's next pronouncement.

"However, Mr. Calhoun, you have an alternative," Goodykoontz said. With his high voice, the solemnity sounded false.

"What's that?" Calhoun asked, peering through the cigarette smoke.

"Do a job for me. For us." He waved his pale hands expansively, taking in the town.

Calhoun's hackles rose. "Speak," he said calmly despite rising anger.

"You may have been aware of some small commotion yesterday?" When Calhoun nodded, Goodykoontz continued. "It was, I'm sad to say, another raid by

Señor Eusibio Sepulveda." He waited for Calhoun to ask who Sepulveda was. Calhoun saw no reason to do so.

"Señor Sepulveda," Goodykoontz said with contempt, "is the leader of a band of Mexican bandits. Jackals they are, each and every one of those seven bas . . . animals."

"And you want me to go get 'em? That it?"

"Yes," Goodykoontz said flatly. "What about it, Mr. Calhoun? Will you take on this small task?"

Calhoun dropped the cigarette butt in the dirt and squashed it out. "What do I get in return?"

"Your sentence will be canceled." That caused a small uproar from the crowd, but Goodykoontz was oblivious to it. He could easily convince these people that if Calhoun was successful, Tubac would no longer have to fear Sepulveda and his horde. If Calhoun was not successful, his fate would be the same as if he had been hanged.

Calhoun thought about it. He could not really turn down the offer, but there were a heap of questions about all this.

"Well?" Goodykoontz asked impatiently. "What will it be?"

"Reckon I can help," Calhoun said evenly. He paused, then added, "If you can answer a few questions."

"Ask them," Goodykoontz said imperiously.

"Here?" Calhoun was surprised.

"Why not? I have nothing to hide."

Calhoun shrugged. "If there's only seven bandits, why haven't your men taken care of 'em already?"

Goodykoontz's pasty face got even more pale.

"The bandits have an uncanny knack of raiding Tubac when most of my employees are off at the mine or elsewhere. I suppose they have informants in town," he said, allowing his anger to grow. "Probably someone among his own people who feels some sort of allegiance to Sepulveda."

"Undoubtedly," Calhoun said sarcastically.

"You have any other questions, Mr. Calhoun?"

"A few."

"I think we can address them later," Goodykoontz said gruffly. "I see no need to subject the people of Tubac to more of the day's heat just to listen to you ask about the technical aspects of this job."

Calhoun shrugged. He didn't much care one way or the other. He knew Goodykoontz wanted to get out of the glare of the citizenry while he answered questions. It was interesting to see the change in the fat man.

Goodykoontz dismissed the proceedings. Then, with the help of Perlmutter and Nighswander, he ponderously labored down from the wagon and headed into his saloon. Calhoun, escorted by his four guards, followed. Goodykoontz sat behind his desk. Droplets of sweat streaked down his smooth, flaccid face to drip onto the suit. He picked up a paper fan and waved it before his face, relishing the breeze it created.

"Sit, Mr. Calhoun," he said after a few moments.

Calhoun did.

"Now, ask your questions, but be careful how you ask them," Goodykoontz warned.

"First, tell your punks back there to take a walk," Calhoun said flatly. "Then give me back my weapons."

"I'll do no such thing, Mr. Calhoun," Goodykoontz said. He sounded offended. "That would be foolish."

Calhoun's eyes deepened. He tensed, preparing for action, and eased his hand behind him. The others still thought he was unarmed. He figured he could get the backup Walker out easily and take care of at least two of Goodykoontz's men. The other two, if they were any good at all, might be able to respond by then, but Calhoun reasoned that the risk was worth it.

Goodykoontz saw the look on Calhoun's face and grew suddenly worried. He was certain the saddle tramp was planning some devilment. "I would have no assurances that you would not try to harm me, if I were to do those things," he said calmly, though hastily.

"You have my word."

Goodykoontz stopped fanning himself and stared at Calhoun. There was death in Calhoun's eyes, Goodykoontz could see that. Calhoun was a man who had killed often, and could do so easily though, Goodykoontz suspected, never lightly. Still, he seemed a man of his word. He had done nothing that he had said he would not. It might be risky, Goodykoontz thought, but he would go along—to a point. He nodded.

"Mr. Perlmutter, let the others out, please," Goodykoontz said. "You will stay." He glanced at Calhoun, who nodded acceptance.

Calhoun did not think Perlmutter was much of a gunman, though he did not want to test his theory. He could see Goodykoontz's dependence on Perlmutter, though, and accepted it. He was satisfied in having Nighswander, Blackie, and Four Eyes out of the room.

"And, Mr. Perlmutter, have one of the men bring in Mr. Calhoun's things. Right away." He looked at his guest. "Anything else, Mr. Calhoun?"

"A drink'd be nice."

Goodykoontz nodded. "Mr. Perlmutter, see to it. I will join him."

Perlmutter poured Calhoun and Goodykoontz drinks and handed them out. Without waiting to be asked, Calhoun half rose and opened the box of cigars on Goodykoontz's desk and took one out. He lit it and puffed after taking a sip of whiskey.

There was a rap at the door, and Perlmutter went to answer it. A man stepped in, handed Calhoun's gun belt, two Dragoons, dirk, and Bowie knife to Perlmutter and then left. Perlmutter carried them to Calhoun and held them out. He said nothing.

Calhoun nodded and stood. He rested the burning cigar on the edge of Goodykoontz's desk, much to the annoyance of the fat man. He took the big knife and hung it around his shoulder. The dirk—a small, pointed dagger—slid into the sheath on the pistol belt. Then he took one of the Dragoons and checked it to make sure it was loaded, and properly. Assured that it was, he shoved it in a holster. He went through the ritual with the second. He buckled on the belt. Satisfied, he picked up the cigar and sat.

"Ask what you will, Mr. Calhoun," Goodykoontz said expansively. He was still sweating heavily, but the fanning was helping.

"Why do you want me to go chasin' after Mexican bandits?" Calhoun asked, blowing out a small, perfect circle of cigar smoke.

Goodykoontz did not answer for some moments. He knew Calhoun was a shrewd man, one not easily fooled by bland words coated with a thin veneer of reality. Then he said slowly, "You are expendable, Mr. Calhoun." He had decided the truth, or most of it anyway, was the best course.

Calhoun nodded. He had more than half suspected Goodykoontz would give him a line of nonsense. He was glad to see it was not so. "I ain't the only one with that qualification."

"Of course not, sir. But you have other qualifications some of those others do not have."

"Such as?" Calhoun finished his whiskey and held out the glass. Perlmutter refilled it.

"Such as the ability to gun down three good pistoleers without even breathing hard. Such as having little to look forward to other than a hangman's noose."

Calhoun nodded again. It all made sense. Still, he figured there must be more to it. "Why don't you just send out your little army after 'em? You got enough guns here to make short work of a small band of bandits."

"Several reasons, the primary one being that such a maneuver would leave Tubac—and therefore me—vulnerable, without protection. Another reason is that those damned Mexican scoundrels know this land well. Too well. If they know an army is after them, they will hole up until my men leave. Or worse, devise an ambush and slaughter my men. Neither is an appealing proposition, sir."

"But you don't much give a shit if I get ambushed?"

"No," Goodykoontz said bluntly. "Besides, with a small group, the bandits might not be aware of you so readily."

Calhoun nodded, having read between the words. "So, I'm not to go on this venture alone, am I?"

"You do not think I'm that foolish, do you, Mr. Calhoun?" Goodykoontz's tiny mouth curled into a little smile.

Calhoun shook his head and downed most of the glass of rye.

"No, sir," Goodykoontz said. "You will be accompanied by Mr. Nighswander, Mr. Blackiston, and Mr. Gates."

Calhoun darkened with anger, but he kept it under wraps. He made himself a mental vow, though, that Four Eyes, if not the others, would not return to Tubac, either at the bandits' hands, or Calhoun's. "Not fond of them boys are you, Mr. Goodykoontz?" he said dryly.

Goodykoontz shrugged, unconcerned. There were few men in his employ that he cared for. Perlmutter was one, possibly the only one. The rest were mere cannon fodder, to be used to the best of their abilities and then cast aside when they had outlived their usefulness.

"What makes you think I won't just shoot 'em and ride off?" he asked.

"There's the matter of Mrs. Viejo," Goodykoontz said quietly. It was a risk, but a calculated one. Goodykoontz was certain that Calhoun cared somewhat for Señora Viejo, especially since Calhoun had killed three men over insults to the woman.

Calhoun nodded. He knew full well Goodykoontz would kill Lucille in a moment if it suited his ends. *It ain't much of a choice,* Calhoun thought, *but it's a lot better than dancing at the end of a hangman's rope.*

"I'll need a horse," Calhoun said.

"You can take your pick of those available."

"And supplies."

"All that you need."

Calhoun nodded again. He polished off the last of his glass of whiskey and stood. "I'll pick out a horse and supplies today. We'll leave in the morning," he said, suddenly in command.

"You'll leave this afternoon," Goodykoontz scolded.

"No." He felt a little satisfaction at the shock on Goodykoontz's face. "I've been in your jail three days. I aim to spend some time with Lucille."

"I can't allow that, Mr. Calhoun. It would be too easy for you to flee."

Calhoun shrugged. "You got boys watchin'. They can stay—outside the house. I catch a one of 'em stickin' his nose inside while I'm there and I'll shoot it off for him, followed by other body parts."

Goodykoontz knew when to call it a day in an argument. He nodded. "Mr. Perlmutter will make any arrangements you need for supplies." His fanning increased as he dismissed Calhoun.

CHAPTER

* 16 *

Calhoun sat astride a flaxen sorrel as he rode slowly out of Tubac. He had gotten the horse the afternoon before, after spending nearly two hours looking animals over. He was not the best judge of horseflesh, but the liveryman told him that this light-colored sorrel with the white mane, tail, and two socks had good bottom and a strong heart. The horse seemed reliable, and Calhoun was tired of looking, so he nodded.

Then he wandered over to Docker's and Meyers', the general store, where he bought whatever he thought he might need for the job. As he had at the livery, he told the men to send the bill to Goodykoontz.

With the three gunmen still following him, tagging him like a calf its mother, Calhoun headed toward Lucille Viejo's. He was more than a little irritated with the unwanted entourage, but there was little he could do about it. When he got to Lucille's, he rapped on the door, then opened it and stepped inside. Four Eyes was barely a step behind, and caught the full force of the wood door in the snout as Calhoun flung it closed behind him. Calhoun had used a little more force than was necessary to shut the door.

Calhoun swung back and jerked the door open. Four Eyes stood there holding his heavily bleeding nose. Nighswander and Blackie stifled laughs.

"Keep your ass outside the house, boy, and you'll have no more of your parts broke," Calhoun threatened. "And warn any others who might come snoopin' around here." He kicked the door shut.

Lucille came up behind him and wrapped her long, strong arms around his middle. She rested her cheek on his broad back a moment. "Put them out of your mind, Wade," she said softly. She was relieved when she felt some of the tenseness drain out of him.

He peeled the woman's hands loose and spread her arms as he turned within their cocoon. She latched them again behind him as he enveloped her and kissed her hard.

"I've been waitin' for you," she finally whispered. Lucille backed up a step and turned. With her arm around his waist, and Calhoun's across her shoulders, they strolled toward the small bedroom.

Throughout the afternoon and evening, Calhoun could occasionally hear Goodykoontz's men outside, giggling and laughing like girls. It irritated him, more because it bothered Lucille than because it bothered him. He paid it little mind, at least after Lucille relaxed next to him.

She, for her part, drew comfort and resolve from Calhoun's quiet, unyielding strength. As long as he was there, she had no fear. It was odd, she thought somewhere in the dusk after they had come together again, that she didn't even really care if any of Goodykoontz's men saw her and Calhoun together.

Normally she would be horrified, but now there was almost a delicious excitement in the thought.

She did wrap herself in a robe, however, when she padded barefoot out to the kitchen to make them supper. They ate quietly, not needing to say anything. No words of love were exchanged. There never had been, and Lucille figured there never would be. She didn't care. She knew what she felt, and was happy to have Calhoun with her.

It was fully dark by the time they had finished eating. While Calhoun rolled a cigarette, Lucille lit two candles in the kitchen area. Soon after, they were back in the small bedroom.

Now there was no noise from outside. Calhoun figured that if Goodykoontz's men were still out there—and he expected at least one or two had been ordered to watch over the house—they were asleep. It was a relief not to hear them. He had not really expected them to cause trouble, but just knowing they were out there, possibly trying to peek inside or listening in, divided his attention at a time he did not want it divided.

He even managed to get a little sleep, entwined in Lucille's arms. She was long and sleek and her skin smoother under his touch than one would imagine looking at her dressed. Then she had a hard, rough look. Relaxed and happy, though, she seemed an almost entirely different being.

Calhoun didn't know what woke him, but he came awake as he always did, instantly alert. He craned his head, listening, looking through the dark. There was nothing untoward in the room, or outside, that he could tell.

His glance fell on Lucille's face. Her eyes were open, watching him. There was no fear in the dark brown orbs, just a peaceful confidence in him, and in the two of them. Lucille smiled somewhat shyly up at him, desire suddenly burning anew in her eyes.

Calhoun almost returned the smile. He felt more comfortable and at peace with Lucille than he had with any woman since Lizbeth had died. That worried him a little, though he would never let on. He bent and kissed her, appreciating her welcoming eagerness.

Somewhere in the next half-hour, he thought he could hear Goodykoontz's men outside. Not until he was done, though, was he aware of hearing the shutters covering one window opening—there was no glass, just an opened space for a window, covered by shutters—creak. He held a finger to his lips, indicating that Lucille should be quiet.

Lucille looked nervous, but then relaxed again. She was still scared, but she was interested in seeing what would happen.

Calhoun heard another sound, and he was sure the shutter moved this time. Since there was no wind outside to push it, he knew it must be someone. He had had enough of these fools leering and chuckling at his expense and, more important, at Lucille's expense. He would not have her ridiculed in such a way.

As he rolled off Lucille, his hand darted toward his Dragoons, which were hanging off the bedpost. Without stopping, he swung around so he was sitting on the edge of the bed, pistol out, and he fired, all in one motion.

Lucille screeched in surprise. An annoyed shout came from outside.

Calhoun rose and glided toward the window. With his left hand, he slammed open the shutter. A startled young man looked up at him, a smile half frozen on his face as the muzzle of Calhoun's Dragoon hovered only inches from his forehead.

"You got something to do, boy? Besides standin' here and dyin', I mean?" Calhoun asked quietly.

It took several seconds for an answer to come. When it did, the voice was dry and scratchy. "I think I can find somethin'."

"Good. I catch you around this window again and I'll put a slug in your head."

The young man backed away, nodding. He gulped, hoping he wouldn't collapse from the weakness in his knees. His ears burned hotly from the laughter of several other men.

Calhoun slammed the shutter closed and hooked the fragile latch. He turned and winked at Lucille. She smiled, a flood of warmth rushing through her. She looked at the hard, strong lines of his naked form, and almost shuddered with a renewed burst of desire.

"Time for breakfast, woman," Calhoun said quietly.

"I like it just where I am," Lucille said. A man had never made her feel like this before, and it both frightened and exhilarated her.

"Git," Calhoun ordered, but there was a softness in the command that had not been present in his voice in years.

Lucille sighed in exaggerated frustration. She flung aside the covers and stood, stretching and yawning. She felt absolutely shameless, but far better about herself than she ever had. She reveled in Calhoun's appreciation—even if he was just faking it—in her presence. Then she pulled on her robe and headed into the kitchen.

Calhoun pulled on his pants, and then broke down the Dragoon he had fired. He cleaned, oiled, and reloaded the pistol, then walked out into the kitchen area. Two cups of coffee sat on the table. Calhoun sat and sipped coffee, and had a cigarette. The aroma of biscuits and spiced eggs and the sizzle of bacon filled the room.

As the food cooked, Lucille came around the table and kneaded Calhoun's neck and shoulders with strong, sure hands.

Soon after, she went back to the stove, and then served the food she had made. They ate quickly and quietly, immersed in their own thoughts. Lucille wondered what Calhoun was thinking. She hoped it was about her, but she figured it probably was on the job he faced.

After another cup of coffee and a final cigarette, Calhoun rose. He rubbed a hand across his face. "Reckon I'd best get movin'," he said. "It'll be dawn before long."

Lucille stood and came around the table. She stood in front of him, placed her hands on his shoulders, and gazed into his eyes. "We got a little time yet," she said. Her throat was dry from fear and desire.

Calhoun looked caringly at Lucille, then nodded. "Reckon we do," he said as he swept her into his arms and carried her toward the bedroom.

* * *

Calhoun was wary as he opened the front door in response to the knock, protecting himself behind the adobe wall. Madison Goodykoontz stood there, filling the doorway.

"Good morning, Mr. Calhoun," Goodykoontz said with a healthy dose of false cheer.

Calhoun grunted. Behind Goodykoontz's bulk, he caught a glimpse of the three men who were to go with him, plus the young man he had threatened the night before, and one other young man.

"I believe it is time you were on your way, Mr. Calhoun."

"Have one of your boys bring my horse around," Calhoun said without apology in his voice.

"Mr. Rasmussen," Goodykoontz said over his shoulder, never taking his eyes off Calhoun. "Go fetch Mr. Calhoun's horse from the livery."

The young man Calhoun did not know spun and left. From the hunched shoulders, Calhoun figured the man was not happy.

"Well, aren't you going to invite me in?" Goodykoontz asked, still trying to portray a pleasantness he did not feel.

"No," Calhoun said flatly.

Goodykoontz's eyes widened and then narrowed in anger. He moved back a step, and Calhoun came out, closing the door behind him. He had already said his good-byes to Lucille.

The day was warm already under the pink, just-past-dawn sky. In the dim light Calhoun could see his three soon-to-be companions standing with their horses. A pack mule waited behind the horses.

"Move, Mr. Goodykoontz," the young man Calhoun had caught the night before said sharply, "and I'll take care of that son of a bitch for you."

"Now, Mr. Woodman, such language . . ."

"Don't matter," Woodman growled. "He shouldn't talk to you that way, and I aim to see him pay for it."

"Don't push your luck, boy," Calhoun commented easily. "You almost crossed the divide last night. Be lucky you're still here."

"Bastard," Woodman breathed.

Goodykoontz stared at Calhoun for a minute. He could see death in the man's eyes, but he moved out of the way anyhow. After all, Woodman would have to face some hard characters in his life. Now was as good a time as any for the young man to test his mettle.

"Make your move, Mr. Woodman," Goodykoontz said. "But, please, wait until I'm quite out of the way." He waddled toward Nighswander, Blackie, and Four Eyes. He stood behind his three gunmen, still able to watch the proceedings, but protected by a wall of human flesh and bone.

As soon as Goodykoontz was fully out of the way, Calhoun could see Perlmutter to his right, at a diagonal. The fastidious aide was leading against a wagon, thumbs hooked in his belt, near his pistol. Calhoun did not think he would interfere, but he would keep an eye on Perlmutter.

Calhoun's gaze had not strayed from Woodman. He had seen Perlmutter out of his peripheral vision. Woodman stood, hand twitching near pistol butt, waiting until Goodykoontz was completely out of the way. Then his hand moved.

CHAPTER

* 17 *

Calhoun calmly plugged Woodman in the chest twice.

The young man jerked as each lead ball hit him. He kind of hung there, seeming to dangle from invisible wires from the sky. But his stance was slack, loose-jointed.

Clem Woodman wondered what was happening. He had felt the balls hit him, but could feel no real pain. He was still standing, too, which was a surprise. Trouble was, nothing worked right. As if in slow motion, he watched his pistol fall out of his hand and send up a small cloud of dust when it landed. The whole world seemed to be moving more slowly than it should, and his vision seemed blurred.

Woodman began to topple, and he found he could do nothing to stop it. Blackness was rushing over him, and was complete before his face slammed into the dusty, rock-strewn earth.

Calhoun stood with smoking pistol in hand, watching for the five seconds or so before Woodman went down in a heap. His eyes, however, were watching Goodykoontz's men, in case one of them wanted to try something. He was not worried about Woodman, knowing that the young man was dead even before he fell.

None of Goodykoontz's men seemed inclined to move, and Calhoun holstered his Dragoon, but left the loop off the hammer.

Goodykoontz waddled up, shaking his frizzle-haired head, though he did not appear to be upset in any way. "You do have a way about you, sir," the fat man said.

Calhoun shrugged. He walked to the shed where his gear was stored. He pulled out his heavy, fancy saddle, bringing it back to the small yard in front of the little portico attached to Lucille's house. He set the saddle down and began reloading his rifle, shotgun, and the two Walkers from the saddle holsters, since there was no telling if the powder was still dry.

When Calhoun finished that, he walked toward the pack mule. Stopping in front of Nighswander, he asked, "Where's my supplies?"

Nighswander jerked a thumb at the mule. "Stowed with the rest."

"Get it."

"That'd be a pain in the ass, man," Nighswander said. His voice was neither angry nor annoyed.

"Time is short, Mr. Calhoun," Goodykoontz said as he toddled up.

Calhoun still stared at Nighswander, who had not broken his gaze away. Then Calhoun nodded, as Rasmussen ambled up on horseback with Calhoun's flaxen sorrel in tow. "First time we break camp," Calhoun warned Nighswander, "I take my own supplies."

Nighswander shrugged, unconcerned. He didn't figure Calhoun was going to live much more than a couple of days. It most likely wouldn't matter how many supplies he had.

Calhoun spun, not liking what he had seen in Nighswander's eyes. He had suspected the man would try something; now he was sure of it. The important thing to learn was when the three would make their play.

Calhoun grabbed his saddle and saddle blanket. Within minutes, he had the sorrel saddled. He pulled himself onto the animal and looked down at Goodykoontz.

"Good luck, Mr. Calhoun," Goodykoontz said. "I wish you well on your excursion. These damned Mexican bandits have become a scourge on this area." His anger seemed to gain steam. "No, more than a scourge, a plague on Tubac and the Santa Rita Mining and Exploring Company."

Calhoun nodded, unmoved by Goodykoontz's agitation. "Just remember what I said about Señora Viejo," Calhoun growled. "One of your men—or anyone else in Tubac—so much as looks at her the wrong way and his head'll be on your desk."

"She will be safe," Goodykoontz promised seriously. "You have my solemn pledge of that."

Calhoun grunted again, not reassured. The words rang hollow to him. For the first time in years, he worried a little about leaving someone behind. He tugged on the reins and the sorrel turned right. He headed out of Lucille's yard, mind already turned to the job ahead. Blackie, Nighswander, and Four Eyes hurried to mount their horses and chase after him.

He turned left on the road, and soon was crossing the

wide arroyo north of town. He swung northwest. Almost immediately, Nighswander trotted up beside him.

"Just where in hell do you think you're goin', Calhoun?" Nighswander asked, an edge to his voice.

Calhoun simply pointed in the direction he had been heading.

"Mexico's that way." Nighswander pointed toward the south, having to twist his body a little to do it.

Calhoun shrugged. "So?"

Nighswander looked at Calhoun as if the man were loco. He shook his head, wondering how Goodykoontz could have put any credence in this man at all. Not that Calhoun was expected to live, but still, Goodykoontz was counting on Calhoun at least finding the outlaws before crossing the divide.

"Well," Nighswander said, as if he were a schoolmarm chastising an errant child, "they *are* Mexican bandits."

Calhoun looked over at Nighswander in annoyance. "Don't mean they're going back to Mexico."

"Where in hell else would they go?" Nighswander asked in exasperation.

"The mines up past Sopori," Calhoun suggested. "Maybe just up into the Sierritas."

"Why?"

Calhoun shrugged again. "Maybe hole up for a spell, till things quiet down." He paused and spit, already hating the dust kicked up by the wind and the horses' hooves. "Maybe raid Arivaca like they did Tubac, head across the mountains to Altar Valley, and then go on down into Mexico."

"Shit," Nighswander muttered. He was aware that he was not brilliant. Goodykoontz told him that frequently enough. Still, Goodykoontz used him because he was reliable and steadfast, if unimaginative. He did not like to have other people see his lack of intelligence or, worse, throw it up in his face like Calhoun had just done.

Nighswander reined up a little, falling back so that he was with his two companions. He knew Calhoun was right, and resigned himself to the thought that Calhoun did not have much longer to live. Indeed, he even considered killing Calhoun now. It would be so easy. He, Blackie, and Four Eyes could draw as one, blasting Calhoun in the back. No one would know, nor care, except perhaps that tall, ungainly woman who had been foolish, or sluttish, enough to have married a damned Mexican.

Nighswander sighed. He would have to wait. As much as he hated to admit it, Calhoun was pretty smart in ways that would help them find the Mexican bandits. Besides, he was mighty good with those Colt Dragoons. That would come in handy once they did find the bandits. Then he would kill Calhoun.

Calhoun did not like riding with the three men behind him, especially since he had seen a promise of death in Nighswander's eyes. He figured, however, that they would wait until he found the bandits before trying to kill him, though he could not be sure of that. He knew Goodykoontz held considerable power over these men, and they generally obeyed his orders.

Out here, though, they might not have any reason to listen to him. It would be an easy matter for them to back shoot him, and leave his body to the buzzards and wolves. They could spend a few days out here and then ride back to Tubac, where they could tell Goodykoontz that the bandits had killed Calhoun. Or that Calhoun had run off.

Calhoun had to rely on fear for a while. The others' fear of Goodykoontz and the considerable power he exercised through this entire area. Fear, too, of what Calhoun was capable of. He knew that Blackie, Four Eyes, and Nighswander were stupid men, and often acted rashly. But they were not fools. They had seen what Calhoun could do, and would know that if they missed him in the first volley, he would be sure to kill at least one of them. None of them would be willing to take the risk of being the one or two who was killed. Or so Calhoun hoped.

Calhoun considered turning on the other three, or at least of plotting their demise. He should be able to manage it with a minimum of trouble and planning. He was not the kind, though, to devise such a cold-blooded scheme. At least not yet.

By midafternoon, they had passed by the mines near Sopori. It was obvious no raids had taken place here, so they did not bother to stop. It did produce a quiet though steady flow of insults from Blackie, Nighswander, and Four Eyes, all directed at Calhoun. They turned southwest, followed the desert trail toward Arivaca.

The epithets and comments stopped, however, when they rode into that town and found that the raiders had been there early the day before. Calhoun wondered what for. The place was small and dusty. It seemed to have no amenities, no reason for anyone to visit. It looked like a poor-man's version of Tubac, and that wasn't saying much.

"Damned greasers come in hell for leather," one man told the four. "Shootin' up the place. Killed Lem Davis and his little daughter. Bastards."

"Which way was they headin'?" Four Eyes asked.

"Northwest. I expect they're headin' for one of those small passes to bring 'em to Altar Valley."

"Let's go, then," Nighswander said. Goodykoontz had not put him in charge, really, but he was used to bossing around Four Eyes and Blackie. He saw no reason not to boss Calhoun around, too.

"No," Calhoun said flatly.

Nighswander turned glittering eyes on Calhoun. "I said we're goin'," he announced.

"Go on ahead," Calhoun said. "I'm stayin' the night here." He looked at the townsman. "There a livery hereabouts?"

The man pointed, and Calhoun nodded. He rode slowly in that direction, leaving three arguing men behind him. By the time the three had arrived at what passed for a livery in Arivaca, Calhoun had unsaddled the sorrel and was currying the animal.

Calhoun left his saddle in the stall by the horse and walked outside. After wandering a little, he found a small restaurant with three tables. He took one and ordered chili and cornbread from the bored, tired waiter. Nighswander, Four Eyes, and Blackie came in just as Calhoun was finishing an after-supper cigarette. He left, ignoring his three traveling companions.

By the time Goodykoontz's three men stumbled back to the livery—three adobe walls, a cactus spine roof, and wood doors for each stall—Calhoun was asleep, having taken over a stall next to the one used by his horse. He half awoke when the three came in, and he lay quietly with a hand on a pistol until the others settled in to another stall several down from his.

Calhoun took his time on the trail the next day, stopping frequently to check for sign of the bandits' passage. The slowly plodding pace and frequent halts elicited a renewed stream of commentary and invective from Goodykoontz's three men.

By late afternoon, they had moved into Altar Valley, and Calhoun had reached the limit of his patience. He kept quiet, and acted no differently than he had before, but he seethed inside as they set up a camp.

"Think you could move a little faster tomorrow, Calhoun?" Four Eyes asked sarcastically.

Calhoun simply glared at him and dished up his salted beef and biscuits. *Your hours are numbered, boy,* he thought. Soon after, he turned in, mind calm now that he had decided what he had to do.

The invective started up again almost as soon as the others threw aside their bedrolls and stood.

"Well, well," Blackie snapped, "you're up. Now, if you can get your ass movin', maybe we can get someplace."

Calhoun punched Blackie in the face, knocking him on his seat into the small flames of the fire.

CHAPTER

✳ 18 ✳

Blackie Blackiston yelled as the hot coals seared his rump a little. He leapt up and began swatting his rear end frantically, trying to brush away the heat and the flickering embers.

"We've had about enough of your goddamn nonsense, Calhoun," Four Eyes snapped as he went for his revolver.

Calhoun promptly shot him dead, sending two lead pellets into Four Eye's heart and lungs. Calhoun whirled a little to his left.

Will Nighswander had unlimbered his Colt pistol and fired off a shot already. The Colt's hammer was back and Nighswander fired again.

Calhoun didn't know where the first two shots went, but he was not about to let Nighswander get off another round. Nighswander might be an addle-brained fool, but Goodykoontz had hired the man for his gun, not his brains. Nighswander was in his element now, steady of hand and eye in the midst of a gun battle. He was crouched, pistol in left hand, thumb sliding the hammer back.

Calhoun popped off two quick shots of his own. The first caught Nighswander in the upper left arm. Nighswander's revolver dropped as his gun arm no longer functioned well enough to keep it in hand. The second missed Nighswander as a bullet from Blackie's Colt hit Calhoun's right thigh, knocking the leg out from under him. Calhoun fell on the knee of that side.

He cranked his torso around and fired the last ball in the Dragoon in his hand. The hasty, unaimed shot punched a hole in Blackie's left shoulder, knocking him back a step. It also threw off Blackie's next shot, which whined off a rock far to Calhoun's right.

Calhoun dropped the Dragoon on the ground at his feet and ripped out the other one. He risked a hasty glance at Nighswander. The wounded gunman was scrabbling in the stony dirt, trying to grab his pistol with his right hand. Calhoun whipped his attention back to Blackie, and fired twice more, aiming this time.

Both bullets ripped into Blackie's guts. The man dropped his pistol and doubled over, groaning. He fell and lay huddled in a fetal heap.

As Calhoun turned back toward Nighswander, a bullet from that man's pistol tore through the collar of Calhoun's shirt, nicking the flesh.

"Shit," Calhoun breathed in annoyance. He fired twice again. One ball punched out Nighswander's left eye; the second shattered his left cheekbone, less than half an inch below the eye.

Nighswander's head was knocked back by the force of the bullets, and he toppled over backward, landing on his back, his left knee in the air.

Calhoun glanced at his own wounded leg. Blackie's bullet had torn a small chunk out of the thigh, though it had not entered it. It should not affect him much. He picked up his empty Dragoon from the ground and holstered it. With the other pistol still in hand, he gingerly stood, trying not to put too much weight on his wounded thigh.

Favoring the leg, he hobbled toward Nighswander, passing Four Eyes's body. Four Eyes had not moved since Calhoun had blasted him, and Calhoun gave the corpse barely a glance as he limped by. Nighswander was dead, too, of course, his face a bloody, broken mess.

Calhoun hobbled over to Blackie. The man was still alive, but was in so much pain that he did not even realize Calhoun was standing over him. Calhoun considered ending the man's suffering with a bullet to the brain, but then decided Blackie did not deserve much sympathy. Calhoun knelt carefully and picked up Blackie's pistol. He tossed it off into the desert.

Leaving the moaning Blackie where he lay, Calhoun shuffled off to the supplies. He got his gun-cleaning kit, a canteen, a bottle of whiskey, and a bandanna. He sat on a small boulder near the fire, where he could keep an eye on Blackie. Half watching Blackie, and occasionally scanning the skyline, he cleaned, oiled, and reloaded the empty Dragoon.

Finished with that, he poured himself a cup of coffee, laced it with some whiskey, and drank a little. Being careful with the gunpowder around, he rolled and lit a cigarette. When he had finished that, and the cup of coffee, he extracted the one unused ball from the other Dragoon, and then cleaned and reloaded that weapon, too. Wiping his hands on his pants, he then stood and put away the powder, ball, and cleaning equipment.

Finally it was time to care for his thigh. He sat back on the boulder, pulled the big Bowie knife, and slit his pants around the wound enough to have some working room. Stretching out the leg, he poured some of the water from the canteen onto the wound. Then he picked up the bottle of whiskey. He gulped several mouthfuls and then poured some of the rye onto the wound. He sucked in a breath involuntarily as the whiskey seared into the raw, bleeding flesh.

Calhoun took two more swigs of the whiskey before setting the bottle back down. He folded the bandanna into a long, thin bandage, wrapped it around the wound, and tied it. He rolled and smoked a cigarette while he waited for the stinging in his leg to subside a little.

Then he began making his breakfast. He took time occasionally to toss a rock at one or another of the half-dozen coyotes that had appeared, drawn by the smell of blood and the promise of fresh meat.

Calhoun ate to the harsh tune of coyotes snapping at each other and the pitiful moaning of the dying Blackie.

When he was done he rolled another cigarette and thought about what he would do. His first inclination was to just pack up his things and ride out. He would be several days gone, at the least, by the time anyone in Tubac found out, if they ever did. Most people there would just assume when the four did not return that he and the others had been slain by the bandits, or possibly by Indians. He was still in Apache country.

He had nothing against Mexicans, or even Mexican bandits. They had done nothing to him, and he had no real hankering to go off chasing them anymore, even though he had given his word that he would find them. That had all changed now that Goodykoontz's men had tried to kill him. He could see no reason for leaving the bodies here and going off chasing the bandits by himself. Let Goodykoontz and the people of Tubac worry about the bandits, he figured.

He had what seemed like a decent horse for a change, enough supplies to last him awhile, and no desire to be where he was. There was little reason for him not to just ride off and forget that he had ever visited Tubac, out here in the farthest western reaches of New Mexico Territory.

He owed no allegiance to Madison Goodykoontz, or anyone else in Tubac. Well, he thought wryly, almost no one. That, however, was the biggest part of his problem. No one in Tubac—including Lucille Viejo—would know that he was not dead. He pulled the cork from the whiskey bottle and downed a slug. *It's time,* he told himself firmly, *to think over just what you think of Señora Lucille Viejo.*

He was not elated at the thought. He had refused for all these years to think about his feelings for any woman. He did not relish doing so now, partly because he was certain he would not like what he would conclude.

He couldn't say that he loved Lucille. That much he was certain of. He was just as certain that he could say that he cared for her more than he had cared for any woman except Lizbeth. The memories of the laughing, red-haired young woman still ate at him after all this time.

He could still see Lizbeth's smiling, beautiful face as she stood on the small porch of their Kansas Territory homestead waving good-bye to him as he had ridden off to lead another wagon train west. She was holding their infant daughter, Lottie, who looked so like her mother already. The sun glinted off the fresh coat of whitewash on the house and on the large barn.

Just as quickly, though, those memories conjured up other, more painful ones: heaps of smoldering rubble where the house and barn had stood. Blood-soaked soil and fresh graves. The knot of rage that sat in his stomach like a pound of rancid bacon. The festering hate that ate at him even now. The infinite sadness at knowing that any chance he had ever had at real happiness had burned away in the fires of his house and barn, and were buried with the brutalized remains of Lizbeth and Lottie.

He had never let another woman get close to him since that had happened. He had made love to more than his share of women, of course, and even knew of some who loved him despite his coldness toward them. But never once in all that time had he let himself go.

Until Lucille Ostergaard Viejo had entered his life little more than two weeks ago. He supposed he had been bushwhacked by her plainness. She was far removed from Lizbeth in beauty and vivaciousness, and maybe he had been unprepared for her. With beautiful women, with those who reminded him of Lizbeth in some way, he was always wary.

But Lucille had been so plain in looks, so even-tempered in her actions, that Calhoun figured he had been caught unawares when he realized how good a woman she was.

"Damn," he muttered. "Damn, damn, damn." He was irritated, mostly at himself. He didn't like this dilemma one little bit.

Once more he thought of just saddling up and riding on, leaving behind the bodies, Madison Goodykoontz and his trouble, and Lucille. He could not afford to give his heart to another. The first time was still too pain-filled, and the mere thought of opening himself to that kind of hurt again was repulsive.

On the other hand, he didn't think he could just leave without her knowing what had happened to him. She had loved him without demand, had sought nothing from him other than a little time and a modicum of decency. She deserved an explanation, even if he just told her he didn't love her and had to ride on. She would understand that, he figured.

Of course, if he never went back, she like most others would figure he had been killed by bandits or Indians. That, he figured, would allow her to go through life thinking he had left still caring for her. It would help her preserve her dignity.

There was one fly in that ointment, he realized with self-loathing at his weakness. He wanted to see her again. Somewhere in the back of his mind was the thought that he could make it work this time, that he could find happiness with the tall, raw-boned, loving woman back in Tubac.

Though he would not let the thought really blossom, he envisioned riding out of Tubac *with* Lucille, and making a home with her someplace.

He poured more whiskey down his gullet, trying to drown the maudlin thoughts in which he found himself wallowing. He was truly disgusted with himself over even considering any of this.

Calhoun swallowed more, and realized he had

drained the bottle, though he was still as sober as a judge. "Shit," he mumbled, tossing the bottle at the coyotes, which had edged a little closer to Nighswander's body. Not that he cared enough about Nighswander to want to keep the coyotes from it. He just had to vent his self-loathing at something, and the coyotes were close at hand.

Calhoun sat long enough to smoke down another cigarette. Then he stood, mind made up. He could not fight what was inside. He would have to go back to Tubac and see Lucille. Then he could deal with it.

He was in no real hurry, however, and the wounded leg was slowing him some. So he took his time as he packed the supplies on the mule. Then came the long, tedious job of saddling four horses. When he had all that finished, he grabbed the nearest body—Four Eyes's—and flung it over the man's horse and lashed it down.

Next he walked Nighswander's horse to his corpse and loaded that. Finally he took Blackie's horse to where Blackie lay. Blackiston had finally succumbed. He must have suffered considerably, Calhoun figured, judging by how long it had taken him to die, and by the frozen look of agony on the face. Calhoun had no sympathy for him.

Wanting to be on the move again, Calhoun swiftly tossed the body across the saddle and tied it down. He kicked some pebbly dirt over the fire, and then carefully pulled himself onto the sorrel's back. He grabbed the rope that led to Nighswander's horse, and then to the two others. He touched his spurs to the flaxen horse's side and moved off slowly.

CHAPTER

✷ 19 ✷

Tubac seemed eerily quiet and empty when Calhoun rode in about midday two days after he had left his camp in Altar Valley. Oh, there were the usual sounds—the ringing of a blacksmith's hammer, wagons clattering up and down the streets, vendors calling out their wares from behind carts under small ramadas, children chattering and running.

Still, something didn't seem right to Calhoun, and he couldn't really put his finger on it. He moved slowly past the side street on which Lucille's house sat. He considered turning up that way and making a quick stop at Lucille's before heading to Goodykoontz's saloon. He knew that would be foolish, however, and so he kept on riding.

People gathered along the side of the dusty track that served as Tubac's main street, lining up in front of some of the dull, flat-roofed adobe houses and businesses. None seemed to be threatening. They all seemed merely curious, though Calhoun thought he could see fear lurking in at least some of them. He figured it was fear of him, since he was riding into town with three dead bodies trailing behind him.

He pulled to a stop in front of Goodykoontz's saloon and slid off the flaxen sorrel. Then he limped into the saloon, and across it, under the watchful eye of two waiters, a bartender, and nearly a dozen worried-looking customers.

Calhoun hesitated a moment before knocking on the door to Goodykoontz's office. He knew he looked a fright, considering that his shirt was coated with blood, as was his right trouser leg. He was filthy, covered with trail dust and several days worth of stubble on his face. He decided he didn't care. He wanted to return Goodykoontz's men to him, and then tell the fat mining superintendent to go to hell. After that he would go to Lucille's, where he could bathe, get a little comfort from the woman, and then decide what to do about him and her. He knocked.

Wary, Perlmutter opened the door and stepped back to let Calhoun in.

"Thank God you've returned, Mr. Calhoun," Goodykoontz said fervently from his accustomed place behind the desk. His face appeared agitated, but otherwise he looked the same as always: fat, finely dressed, smelling of lime water, pudgy hands resting on the mountain of gut.

Calhoun shrugged. He looked at Perlmutter. "Get me a drink, boy."

Perlmutter glanced at Goodykoontz, who nodded. He went to get the whiskey.

Calhoun hobbled to the desk and helped himself to a cigar. He lit it with a match and tossed the match into a cuspidor.

"Where's Mr. Nighswander?" Goodykoontz suddenly asked. "And the others?"

"Outside," Calhoun said evenly. He paused a

moment, then added, "Lyin' across their saddles."

Goodykoontz's eyes widened in surprise. "What happened?" he asked after Calhoun had taken the glass of whiskey proffered by Perlmutter.

Calhoun swallowed the contents of the glass, handed it back to Perlmutter, and said, "Fill it." He looked back at Goodykoontz. "We caught up with them damn bandits a few days ago. Out past Arivaca. They was hidden up among the rocks on a hillside. We was out in the open." He stopped. He was not given to talking much, and he had about reached his limit for one breath.

"So what happened?" Goodykoontz asked in some exasperation.

"They opened fire on us," Calhoun said, glibly continuing the lie. "Blackie and Four Eyes went down right off. I took a ball in the leg." He pointed. "Me and Nighswander flattened out on the ground and shot back. Don't know if we got any of 'em or not." He ran out of steam again and stopped. He took a couple puffs on the cigar, and then a long pull at the glass of whiskey.

"Well?" Goodykoontz asked. He had little patience at the moment. He simply wanted the story told as quickly as possible.

"The firin' stopped after a spell. We waited, but Nighswander got itchy and stood up. Somebody put two bullets in his face for him."

"Damn." Goodykoontz had no real affection for any of his men—except possibly Perlmutter. He did appreciate a good hand when he saw one, though, and Nighswander had been good with a gun, if not endowed with much intelligence. He had been loyal, too, and would be hard to replace.

"I hadn't moved none," Calhoun said after draining his glass and holding it out for a refill. "Once dark come, I managed to gather up the horses pretty quick, got your three men across 'em, and ride out. Stopped sometime yesterday to get some shuteye, and then rode on in here."

Goodykoontz nodded. "And their bodies are outside?" he asked.

"Yep." Calhoun sipped from his refilled glass.

Goodykoontz nodded again, thinking. He was not at all sure that Calhoun wasn't lying to him, though the story certainly sounded plausible enough. He wondered why Calhoun had bothered coming back. He had been a reluctant bandit pursuer at best. With Goodykoontz's three men dead, he could've easily just rode off and never have been seen again. No one would have been the wiser.

It was because of that, though, that Goodykoontz mostly accepted the explanation. There was no reason at all why Calhoun should have come back here—except maybe the woman. Goodykoontz realized, however, that Calhoun could easily have slipped into Tubac under the cover of darkness and took the woman. Goodykoontz sighed. *It's time to get out,* he thought.

"Why didn't you bury them and go after the bandits again?" Goodykoontz asked shrewdly.

Calhoun finished off the whiskey again, but this time he set the glass down on the corner of the desk. "I ain't no goddamn grave digger," he said calmly. "And except that they took a few potshots at me, I got nothin' against them bandits, neither."

"You do now," Goodykoontz said smugly.

Calhoun looked at him through narrowed eyes. The man's face appeared to him to be gloating. "What's that mean?" he asked harshly.

Goodykoontz pursed his tiny mouth for a moment. "While you were gone, Señor Sepulveda paid us another visit, Mr. Calhoun," he finally said.

"And?" Calhoun didn't like the sound of this. Goodykoontz seemed almost to be having a good time, as well as gloating. It didn't seem right for a man whose town had been hit by bandits twice in less than a week.

"And," Goodykoontz said, forcing a look of sincere solemnness onto his flabby, pink-cheeked face, "I'm afraid . . . well . . ."

Calhoun felt like his heart had just fallen out. "Lucille's dead?" he asked in a cold, flat voice.

"No, no, no," Goodykoontz said soothingly. "She is alive. Or at least she was when she was last seen." He managed to keep the smirk off his face.

Calhoun, whose relief had been fast and overwhelming, found his renewed heart sickness as immediate in returning. "She was taken?" he asked with a bitter edge to his voice.

Goodykoontz nodded.

"Why her?" Calhoun asked harshly. Rage burned inside him, and he wanted to lash out at someone, something. He didn't care who or what. He managed to keep his temper from exploding only with a tremendous effort.

"It was not directed at you, I'm sure, Mr. Calhoun," Goodykoontz said unctuously. "She was not the only woman taken. Nearly a dozen were dragged off by those scoundrels." He shook his head, expressing a disbelief and annoyance he didn't really feel. At least not at the fact that the women had been kidnapped. He was, however, less than pleased at the raids.

"I don't give a damn about the others," Calhoun snapped.

Goodykoontz shrugged. "They were all Mexicans anyway," he said. "Except for Señora Viejo, who was almost one of them."

Calhoun did not let the gibe annoy him. He was still too enraged by the fact that not only had Sepulveda raided the town, but had carted off his woman. "When was this?" he asked, teeth clamped tightly on the cigar.

"Saturday."

"So they've had three days' head start," Calhoun said, almost as if speaking to himself. "Heap of time."

"They're probably well into Mexico by now," Goodykoontz said softly. He paused, gloating to himself. "Are you going after them?" he finally asked.

Calhoun only nodded. Anyone who knew him, even a little, would not need an answer to such a question.

"When will you leave?"

Calhoun wanted to head out this very minute, but he was tired from the traveling and sore from his wound. Moreover, though, the sorrel had been used hard and would need a little time to recover.

"Mornin'," he said. He straightened. "I need some supplies and such."

"Get anything you need over at Docker's and Meyers'," Goodykoontz said magnanimously.

Calhoun nodded. "I'll pick most of it out. You have someone pack it on the mule and have it and my horse—saddled—out in front of Señora Viejo's place before dawn."

"It'll be done. You want some riders with you this time?"

"No." The word was ugly in its flatness and harshness.

"You'll take on all seven of them?" Goodykoontz was not surprised, nor displeased. The bandits had nothing he could live without, except some money, most of which was not his anyway. He would hate to lose any more men. At the same time, he did not mind if Calhoun was killed. Calhoun riding out alone would suit Goodykoontz's purposes very well.

"Yep." The word rang of death; bloody, violent and certain death.

"Anything else I can do for you, Mr. Calhoun?" Goodykoontz asked.

"Keep your fat ass and your men out of my way."

Goodykoontz nodded, his face looking offended at Calhoun's words and orders.

Calhoun spun and stalked out of the room, the pain in his leg nearly forgotten. His spurs jingled loudly in the deadly silent saloon. Outside, he shoved angrily through the crowd that had gathered around the horses. He mounted his flaxen sorrel and rode toward the livery, leaving the corpse-bearing animals and the mule tied to the hitching rail.

At the livery he turned the horse in. "Care for him good, Morales," he snarled. "He's been hard used and deserves good."

"Sí," Juan Morales said, nodding. He was not obsequious around Anglos, like many of the other Mexican inhabitants of Tubac were. He was a proud man, and held himself that way.

"And watch that saddle, boy. I find so much as a scratch on it and I'll stomp your ass into the ground."

"Sí," Morales said. He sounded bored, and unafraid. He knew Calhoun would do as he had said. Morales also knew that Calhoun knew that he did not need to be told to guard the saddle.

"Have him saddled before dawn. One of Goodykoontz's ass kissers'll be along to get him and bring him to me."

Morales nodded. "You are going after Sepulveda?" he asked.

"Yep." He turned and, carrying his saddlebags, walked off, trying not to limp as he headed to Docker's and Meyers' store. He bought supplies, but took only a few things with him to Lucille's place.

In the house he built a fire and cooked some food, which he ate without much enjoyment.

Afterward, he cleaned his pistols, the rifle, and the shotgun. Once they were cleaned and greased, he reloaded them. When he was done with that, he loaded four extra cylinders for the big Walkers he carried in holsters on the saddle. He placed caps on the nipples, holding them in place with a dab of grease. He did the same with four extra cylinders for the Dragoons. Then he made sure he had enough paper cartridges in the pouch on his belt.

Finally he cleaned up the mess, washed up as best he could in a basin, and then stripped off his worn, bloody clothes. He tossed them aside, and then washed off his wound and rebandaged it with a new bandanna.

He crawled into bed at last. Shutting any thought of Lucille out of his mind, he fell asleep almost instantly.

CHAPTER

✳ 20 ✳

Perlmutter and Rasmussen, the young man who had been at the house the last time Calhoun left, were waiting in Lucille's yard when Calhoun stepped outside. Perlmutter held the reins to Calhoun's saddled sorrel; Rasmussen had the mule's rope in hand.

Calhoun threw his saddlebags over the cantle and pulled himself on the sorrel. He leaned over and took the rope to the mule.

Perlmutter looked up at him. "Mr. Goodykoontz asked me to tell you that he is most displeased with this turn of events, and that those who are responsible must be punished to the utmost."

Calhoun nodded. "You know which way they were headed?"

"Southeast, though that doesn't mean they kept going that way. Fort Buchanan is in that direction."

"I'm aware of that," Calhoun said dryly.

"Find them, Mr. Calhoun. Find them and punish them," Perlmutter added solemnly.

Calhoun did not think Perlmutter's remark required an answer, and he certainly had nothing to say to Rasmussen, so he tugged at the sorrel's reins and headed off down the dusty street.

Tubac was still quiet, as its residents had not

awoke yet for the most part. Cocks crowed, the sound harsh and sharp, carried on the light, stuffy breeze. The animals' hooves sent up small but tenacious puffs of dust that rose to invade Calhoun's nose and mouth.

Calhoun clomped slowly up the silent streets and then turned southeast on the road that eventually would lead to Fort Buchanan. He was glad in some ways to be leaving Tubac behind him, but he was pressed by a rising sense of urgency. Eusibio Sepulveda and his band of cutthroats were not the type of men to treat captive women kindly. And with almost four days' head start, Calhoun did not hold out much hope that the women would not have been abused.

For himself, Calhoun didn't much care if Lucille had been used by those men. He would still care for her. However, he had seen what such treatment often did to women, and Lucille might want nothing to do with him if she had been abused by Sepulveda's band. And the longer she was with them, the more likely it was that she would have been abused beyond all reason.

He pushed on, not going too fast, but not delaying either. As he rode, he tried to keep thoughts of Lucille from crowding into his mind. Too many such thoughts would not allow him to keep his mind on the job he would soon face.

It was pretty well light now, and he would be able to read sign—if there was any to read. He was sure Sepulveda and his men would not continue on this road very far. Not with an American fort twenty-five miles away, and the Mexican border maybe the same distance south.

He slowed a little, wanting to make sure he spotted the place where they left the road and headed across country. He did not think they would head toward the Santa Rita Mine and raid it. If they had not been dragging the women along with them, that would have been far more likely, but since they were, they would be fools to try such a stunt.

The road curved due east where a small creek flowed into the Santa Cruz River. Late in the day, surprised that he had seen no trail cutting off the road, Calhoun came to the spot where he had killed the three Apaches. Shrugging, he pulled into the thicket of mesquite and acacia.

There was no sign of his earlier battle. The only signs that anyone had been there before were those of old campsites—a well-used fire pit, scraps of firewood, the flotsam of men none too neat in their camping.

He unsaddled the sorrel and unloaded the mule. He gathered wood, built a fire, and tossed some salted beef in a frying pan over the flames, then added a coffeepot to the fire. He rolled a cigarette and smoked it while he waited for his meal to be ready.

After he ate, he smoked another cigarette, and pondered things. He had been sure Sepulveda and his men would have cut off the Fort Buchanan road by now. But he had seen nothing, and he could not have missed it if seven men, a dozen women, and two dozen or more horses had cut cross-country across the rolling, rocky land.

He had stopped for almost half an hour where the road to the Santa Rita Mine cut north, and he had searched till his eyes were bleary. There had been plenty of traffic—horse and wagon—over the past several days, but nothing that would lead Calhoun to believe a band of bandits, carting a passel of women, had passed that way.

Calhoun finally turned in, worried about Lucille, and wondering if he would ever be able to find Sepulveda's men. He slept, but it was none too refreshing. In the morning he made a hasty breakfast and then began preparing to leave.

Once back on the trail, he stifled his urge to gallop. All that would accomplish would be to wear down the horse. He would see no sign by doing that, and he could easily be ambushed. So he forced himself to keep a slow, steady pace, one that would allow him to scan the ground, the horizon when there was one, the stunted, gnarly trees and other sparse vegetation.

He was beginning to think Goodykoontz had sent him on a wild-goose chase. So pressing did the thought become that he stopped in the middle of the road and worked it over in his mind while he smoked a cigarette.

He had no real proof that Sepulveda and his men had raided Tubac again, other than Goodykoontz's word for it, and the seemingly stunned look on the faces of the populace. Nor could he figure why Goodykoontz would send him out here, unless Goodykoontz was just dead set on seeing the bandits dead. Even if that were true, though, Goodykoontz had enough men at his disposal to be more certain that the job would be accomplished.

It was possible, he supposed, that Goodykoontz just wanted him dead, but that still did not make any real sense out of this. He had already sentenced Calhoun to hang, and, again, had enough gunmen that he could send against Calhoun to ensure the job.

Calhoun had the suddenly horrifying thought that Goodykoontz had concocted this story simply to get at Lucille, for some unknown reason. He could have been holding Lucille prisoner in any of a number of places around town. That didn't make much sense, either, since Calhoun could not fathom any reason at all that Goodykoontz would have for doing it.

Still, it left a cold, hard feeling inside of him. Because of that, Calhoun told himself that he would ride as far as Fort Buchanan. If he did not find anything before then, he would turn around and go back. He also vowed that when he got back to Tubac, he would beat some answers out of Goodykoontz, and Perlmutter, if necessary.

With his mind resolved, though with no relief, Calhoun pushed onward. He did experience some hope, however, when he saw some fairly fresh sign breaking off to the southeast again.

He stopped, and with pounding heart examined the tracks. He could not be sure, but he suspected it was Sepulveda and his band. A few of the hoofprints looked familiar, though it was hard to tell anything for sure in this soil, which was either too dusty or too rocky, depending on where one was at any particular time.

Calhoun did some calculating, and figured he was less than two miles from Fort Buchanan. He did not know the area ahead, but there were small mountains to the south, and he figured that Sepulveda would know a trail that would take him around the mountains.

Calhoun nodded and climbed back onto the horse. He spurred the animal and trotted off, kicking up more dust than he was comfortable with. He needed speed, though, if he wanted to catch Sepulveda before too long.

The trail, if that's what it could be called, crossed Sonoita Creek. It took Calhoun nearly twenty minutes of searching before he picked up the track again across the stream. He finally did, a mile or so downstream. He hurried on, following the signs sharply southeast, in the wide saddle of desert between the Patagonia Mountains to the west and the Canelo Hills to the east. Beyond the hills were the more formidable Huachuca Mountains.

He made his camp late in the afternoon amid a patch of mesquite, acacia, and cactus beside which trickled a thin thread of water. It was enough for him to make coffee and for the animals to drink their fill— if they didn't do so all at once. The sun had dipped behind the crest of the Patagonias, and though it was still light, the shadows made tracking difficult.

The arrival of nightfall did little to relieve the heat. Calhoun found it oppressive, and he was almost desultory in making his small camp. He did not really want to eat because of the temperature, but knew he had to. So he forced himself to make a small fire and cook. He ate without enthusiasm.

He wanted to be on the move again. He sensed he was closing in on the bandits, and he wanted it over with. He also wanted Lucille back, safe and sound. He no longer worried about what he felt for her. It was enough to know he cared for her and wanted her with him. He would deal with his past and the memories as best he could when he thought the time was right.

As he stretched out on his bedroll, he wondered how far ahead of him Sepulveda was. He figured the outlaw to be in Mexico. The question was how far. Calhoun cared not a whit about following the bandits into Mexico. The border meant absolutely nothing to him. Nor did the fact that he would be a stranger among the people of Mexico, people who more than likely would be happy to protect the bandits, as well as see him killed.

Morning offered no hope for relief from the heat. As Calhoun prepared his simple breakfast, he continually wiped the sweat from his forehead. He decided, as he smoked a cigarette after his meal, that when he got Lucille back, he would take her away from here. He didn't much care where, as long as it was a place that was cool as often as not, and one where there might be a possibility for rain of a time. He sure wouldn't stay in this hell's furnace.

He made certain the horse and the mule were well watered, and that his canteen was full before he pulled out. He wasn't sure how long it would be before he found more water, and he was not about to be out here on foot, trying to find bandits and water both.

Late in the afternoon, the sound of gunfire brought him to a stop. He sat there, listening to the far-off sound and trying to figure out exactly where it was coming from. He couldn't place it, so he rode on slowly, stopping occasionally to listen some more.

The gunfire was sporadic, as if one group had another pinned down. He saw a narrow canyon to his left. It headed into the not-very-tall Canelo Hills. On a hunch, he moved into the canyon. Almost immediately the gunfire's loudness increased, and Calhoun knew he was on the right track.

He slowed, and then stopped when he saw the puffs of gun smoke from the hills. He went to his right and dismounted. Then he secreted the horse and the mule in what was little more than a wide crack in a rock cliff. He tied both animals to a creosote bush that grew out of the side of the stone, and pulled off his spurs. He dropped those in one of his saddlebags and then he headed out on foot, Henry rifle in hand.

Calhoun crept past boulders, around stunted, wind-twisted trees, and jumbles of fallen rock. The land rose, and Calhoun slowed his pace even more, figuring that the attacking force, whom he figured to be a band of Apaches, was on the heights.

He stopped and watched for the puffs of smoke, trying to get a fix on where the Indians were. When he had several placed in his mind, he moved on again. He was moving hardly at all, inching his way along, when he spotted a patch of color that did not belong in the stark, cactus-covered hills. He headed that way.

The Apache was concentrating on the scene before him, and not paying much attention to anything else. Calhoun realized that the Apaches might be attacking someone other than the bandits, but he decided he didn't care. After what the Apaches had tried to do to him a couple of weeks ago, and considering how he felt about Indians in general, he was willing to help whoever was being attacked.

With eyes narrowed in hate, Calhoun crept up on the unsuspecting Apache.

CHAPTER

* 21 *

The Apache, who was crouching behind a boulder and a screen of scraggly brush, never had a chance. As Calhoun neared the warrior, he lay down his rifle and slid out the large, wicked Bowie knife, then crept ever closer to the Indian.

The Apache had just fired off his single-shot rifle and was beginning to reload when Calhoun slipped up behind him. As the warrior pounded a ball down the barrel with the ramrod, Calhoun's left hand wrapped around the Indian's mouth and jerked his head backward. The other hand slid the razor-sharp Bowie roughly across the Apache's throat.

Blood spurted, and the warrior struggled for a few moments before death overtook him. Without moving his left hand, Calhoun wiped the knife blade on the Apache's cloth shirt and then slid the weapon into the sheath.

Still holding his hand around the lower portion of the Indian's face, Calhoun half rose and dragged the body a few feet away and dropped it. Then he retrieved his rifle and took the Apache's place behind the rock and thin, withered brush.

Calhoun surveyed the scene. People were huddled behind wagons down in one of the interminable dips in this harsh, stark land. There was a small spring, which would provide a little water. Three small oaks—Calhoun figured them to be shrub oaks— were close to the spring. Other vegetation, except for short, brown grass and a sprinkling of sagebrush and various cacti, was nearly nonexistent.

The slight hollow was maybe a hundred yards from where Calhoun squatted, and about the same from anywhere else up on the surrounding hills that might give someone a vantage point. It was, for the most part, Calhoun thought, a good place to hole up for a few days. It was out of the way, had water and a little wood, and was probably as safe a place as one could find in Apache country.

Calhoun was not sure the people were the bandits he was pursuing, but he was certain they were not simply innocent travelers, either. Those wagons were not loaded with supplies, or home goods, or anything else. They were loaded with booty. Calhoun assumed they had gotten the wagons in their raid on Tubac.

He counted seven men, all wearing sombreros. He could tell little else about them at this distance. He also saw some women, but he could not pick out Lucille, or anyone else he might have seen in Tubac.

The group looked pretty well fortified behind the wagons. They had plenty of food, Calhoun surmised, and they had water, so they could last a while. The land for almost a hundred yards in any direction was open, so the Apaches would be reluctant to rush the camp, since that would mean taking heavy losses. Unless the Apaches had a large force, which was doubtful, the Mexicans down below could hold out almost indefinitely.

The only trouble the Mexicans seemed to be having was in controlling the horses and mules. Most of the animals were tied to the small oaks. A few others were tied to the sides of the wagons. Two of the men moved among the animals every few minutes, trying to calm them.

Remaining behind his cover, Calhoun scanned the hills all around as best he could, trying to spot where the Apaches were hidden. He could not see them, but he did spot puffs of gun smoke and even arrows on occasion.

After almost a quarter hour of watching, he figured there were nine, maybe ten Apaches left. He squatted awhile longer, trying to figure out how best to approach his task. He had to either kill the Apaches or send them packing in order to have the bandits to himself—if they were the bandits. If they weren't, he still thought it a good idea to disperse the Apaches.

Problem was, removing nine or ten Apache warriors was not a job one undertook lightly. They were hard, tough men, and in their element out here in this stark, harsh mountain desert. He sighed. *No, he thought, it won't be easy. But it's got to be done.*

Calhoun scanned the landscape again, taking another five minutes or so. He saw nothing different from last time. He counted no more Apache positions than he had before, and none had moved. He rose and moved off quietly, rifle in his left hand, one of his Dragoon pistols in his right, thumb on the hammer.

* * *

It was easier than he had figured it would be, though it took a considerable amount of time and stealth. The first two Apaches he snuck up on and knifed to death had been so easy that Calhoun wondered about the reputation Apaches had.

Finally, he realized that they had reason to be lax. First off, there was the gunfire that popped with some regularity. Secondly, the Apaches simply never suspected that anyone—least of all one silent, deadly individual—would come up from behind. There were no towns anywhere near here; Fort Buchanan and the Santa Rita Mine were miles away. There had been no pursuit, so the Apaches were comfortable in not watching their backs.

Calhoun also assumed that part of his ease in creeping up on the Apaches was their arrogance. From all that he had heard, and seen, of these warriors, they would not believe that anyone could do that to them. Their reputation was so fierce and had spread so wide that they thought themselves invincible to such attack.

Calhoun killed another Apache with his knife, and then pressed on, moving as stealthily as he could. Though it had seemed easy, sneaking up on the Apaches was difficult. In these desert mountains, there was little vegetation large enough to hide behind, and what there was of it was generally clumped together. The only cover available with any regularity were the rocks. Without them, Calhoun's job would have been impossible.

It was then that he almost stumbled right into the small camp the Apaches were using as a base for this attack. Only the sound of several horses kept Calhoun from wandering into the camp, unsuspecting. Had he heard only one horse, he would've been cautious and moved ahead, thinking that a warrior had tied his horse to a tree while he was attacking. But several in the same area made his senses perk up.

He peered through the tall, spindly arms of an ocotillo around which a thin bush was growing. Three Apaches sat around a fire, drinking coffee, talking, and frequently laughing. A dozen horses were picketed to a rope tied between two mesquite trees.

Calhoun watched for a while. He had wondered earlier where the Apaches' horses were, since he had seen none near any of the warriors he had killed. While the Apaches were not Plains warriors, and so not as accustomed to living on horseback as were those peoples, they would not travel such great distances without animals unless they were forced to. Now he knew where they were.

He cursed himself silently for not having realized this must be the case before. And for having almost walked into his own death because he was not thinking. He had begun to feel that the Apaches, being none-too-vigilant right now, were easy pickings.

As Calhoun watched, another warrior walked into the camp and said something in a harsh, guttural language. The four Apaches laughed. The latest arrival squatted by the fire and poured coffee. Like all the others Calhoun had seen, he wore a colorful cloth headband holding his shoulder-length black hair in place. They also wore breechcloths, some of buckskin, some of cloth, and moccasins rolled up to the thighs. The moccasins, Calhoun noticed, had toes that were pointed and curved up and back around toward the foot. The warriors' shirts also were of cloth or buckskin.

Calhoun knew it would be folly to attack this camp. He was good with a gun, but he was not at all sure he could take down the four of them before he bought the farm himself. Moreover, there might be others nearby. He decided he had better leave the camp alone, at least for now, though the thought of cutting the horses loose and sending them fleeing was tempting.

He backed away, slowly and cautiously. When he was some yards away, he stopped and mopped his sopping forehead with a bandanna. It was hellaciously hot. He wiped his hands on his pant legs, wincing a little when his hand rubbed over the bandanna that still covered the wound on his thigh, and he moved on.

All this creeping around and squatting to wait for the right moment to attack was placing a severe strain on his wounded thigh, which was beginning to ache considerably.

Minutes later, he was moving up on another Apache. Then his foot hit a loose rock and twisted under him. He fell hard on his right hip. If the sound of his fall wasn't enough to alert the warrior, his involuntary grunt of surprise would have.

The Apache cranked his head around. When he saw Calhoun, the dark eyes in the scowling face widened.

He swung around, coming to his feet in the same motion. He cast aside his bow as being useless at such a short distance. He ripped out his wood-handled knife and charged, raising the knife over his head.

"Shit," Calhoun breathed in annoyance at his clumsiness. He was lying on his gun hand, and couldn't quite get the Dragoon up enough to shoot the Apache. He dropped the rifle in his left hand, and began pushing himself up on his right hand.

The rushing warrior was almost on him, and he surged halfway up to his feet. He drove his shoulder into the warrior's pelvis and wrapped his hands around the tops of the Apache's thighs in the back. He pushed all the way up to his feet, dumping the warrior up and over his shoulder.

The Apache landed hard on the upper part of his back, but he made no sound. By the time the Indian got to his knees and was shoving upward, Calhoun had brought the pistol to bear on him. He hesitated only long enough to decide he could not afford not to shoot the Indian. He fired once.

The warrior was knocked backward by the power of the .44-caliber ball hitting him in the bridge of the nose. His hand jerked and twitched, as if trying to grasp a weapon.

Calhoun swept up his rifle and ran. Moments later, several arrows clinked off rocks around him, and at least one bullet whined off a boulder to his right, spraying him with shards.

He skidded and slid to a stop a few yards farther on behind another large rock. He swiftly checked to make sure the cap was still on his rifle. Then he brought the Henry up across the rock and waited. Moments later, an Apache popped up from behind another boulder fifty yards away. Calhoun fired.

The Apache disappeared. Calhoun wasn't sure he had hit the Indian, though from the way the Indian had gone down, he was fairly certain he had. He swiftly reloaded, working mostly by feel, with a paper cartridge pulled from a pouch on his gun belt. The one Apache never showed himself again.

Another did, though, several feet to the first one's right. This one used a rifle to let fly a shot in Calhoun's direction. Calhoun could see the warrior toss the rifle away. Moments later the warrior fired an arrow at Calhoun, who felt pretty safe behind the boulder.

Reloaded, with a fresh cap on the nipple of the cocked Henry rifle, Calhoun waited again, sighting down the rifle, which rested across the boulder.

The wily Apache was not showing himself now. Calhoun knew he could either wait, hoping that none of the other Apaches would find him. Or he could be off and moving, hoping that the Indian he had shot at was dead, or severely wounded enough not to be able to stop him. And that the second one had moved off. It was not an easy choice to make, and the wrong decision could prove fatal in a real hurry. He decided to wait just a bit yet, to see what developed.

C H A P T E R

* 22 *

Suddenly an arrow appeared in Calhoun's rifle stock, less than two inches from the tip of his nose, and within a hairbreadth of where his right thumb and fingers almost came together wrapping around the stock.

"Damn," he snapped. He jerked the rifle up and around. He didn't see the Apache as much as sense some form of movement. He fired and saw something fall. He wasn't sure what.

He knew he could not stay here much longer, though. He jumped up and ran, heading toward a jumble of boulders to his left. He made it, though not without being fired at several times with arrows.

Calhoun knelt behind the rocks, breathing heavily. He wiped sweat from his face and forehead, feeling more dribbling down his sides, stomach, and back beneath his new shirt. "Damn heat," he mumbled as he stuffed the bandanna back into his pocket.

He wrenched the arrow out of his rifle and threw it angrily aside. "Damn Apaches." He began reloading the Henry. Twice while he was doing so, arrows clattered against the rocks. Both seemed to have been fired by the second Apache.

Calhoun nodded as he came up with the germ of

an idea. He slid the Henry over a rock and rested it there. Then he flattened on the ground and gently placed his worn old slouch hat on the rock, too, next to the rifle. He slithered off, heedless of the rocks that gouged his legs and stomach.

Ten yards to his left, and somewhat on a diagonal, he stopped and peered around a rock. He was not satisfied with the view, and he moved off, stopping again and peering around a rock. He nodded and pulled a Dragoon. He cocked it and held it out at arm's length. "Stick your nose out now, you son of a bitch," he muttered.

The Apache finally obliged. He did not come up over the boulder, but rather around the side of it. The side of which Calhoun now had an unobstructed view.

Calhoun fired with a sense of satisfaction. He was satisfied not because he had killed the warrior, but because he had outwitted him. He sort of duck-walked toward where he had left the rifle. He found his hat several feet behind the boulder, an arrow through it. The arrow had caught the hat and brought it along on its flight, which ended when the arrow hit a rock and broke.

Uncocking the rifle, Calhoun stood, risking death. He knew he could not crawl around forever. No one shot at him. He turned and began making his way cautiously toward the Apache camp.

He stopped and knelt behind a boulder just outside the camp. He waited patiently, watching. Their horses were still there, but he saw no warriors. Still, he was wary. The Apaches had shown themselves to be far too tricky for his liking.

Calhoun crept around the perimeter of the camp, more than once having to move quickly across the spot that offered no cover. He spotted no one, though, and he began to wonder where the other warrior who had been in the camp had gotten off to. He had no way of knowing for sure, but he hoped the Indian had gone off to join his companions.

Of course, if the warrior had done that, Calhoun thought wryly, he was going to be neck deep in Apaches any minute now. He decided he had better hurry. Besides, he was getting tired of all this slinking around.

He boldly strode to the rope between the two mesquite trees, to which the horses were picketed. He leaned the Henry against the mesquite, pulled the Bowie with his right hand, and grabbed the rope in his left hand.

Just as he was about to slice the rope, something hit him hard in the back, knocking his hat off. He had the thought as he went sprawling, knife flying out of his hand, that he hoped he had not been shot. He landed hard on his face, then bounced on his nose. Something landed on him, and he knew he had not been shot.

"Son of a bitch," he snarled under his breath as a hard, callused hand grabbed his hair and began jerking his head back. Calhoun knew what that meant. He shoved up onto his hands and knees with all his might, feeling the Apache sliding down off his back a little. The move freed his arms just in time to stop the knife in the dark bronze hand from slitting his throat.

Ignoring the flash of pain from his wounded thigh, Calhoun pushed up using only his leg strength, while he kept both hands clamped on the Indian's knife hand.

Suddenly he felt the Apache's teeth on his left ear. He sucked in his breath. Holding the knife hand in his own right, he balled up his left hand, leaving the thumb knuckle extended. He jerked the fist backward over his shoulder several times, hoping to hit the Indian's eye with the thumb joint. He did on the fourth time, though with each earlier blow, his knuckle had cracked on the warrior's forehead.

The Apache let go of Calhoun's ear as he yanked his head back away from the still-probing fist.

It took a moment for Calhoun to realize the Indian's head was no longer where it was. He snapped his left hand back onto the Apache's hand just below the wrist and shoved outward, while at the same time jerking the Indian's forearm forward. The Apache's wrist snapped, and the knife fell.

Though the Indian made no sound even as his bones broke, Calhoun knew he was not out of danger yet. He shoved the Apache's broken arm away from him, then snapped his right elbow backward as hard as he could. He felt a sharp little pain in the elbow, but knew that he had cracked at least one of the Indian's ribs.

Calhoun took two steps forward and spun. The Apache had grabbed his knife in his left hand and was already coming at him.

"Damn, boy, you don't know when to give up, do you," Calhoun muttered rhetorically. He fell to his left side, and the charging Indian rushed by. Calhoun scrambled up and pulled one of the Dragoons as the Apache turned and faced him.

The warrior's small dark eyes were enraged. He seemed to be feeling no ill affects from his broken arm. He snarled something in his own language. Calhoun could not understand any of it, but he knew it was not meant as a greeting.

Calhoun spit into the dirt. He was fed up with Apaches and the desert, and the heat and Mexican bandits and Madison Goodykoontz. Calhoun thumbed back the hammer. The Apache took a step toward him. "Try this you dumb red son of a bitch," Calhoun snapped. He shot the Apache square in the chest.

Before the Indian had crumpled, Calhoun had shoved the Dragoon back into his holster, whirled, and sought out his knife. The ponies watched him, rolling their eyes nervously. They did not like his white man's scent, and there had been too much activity here in the past few moments.

Calhoun grabbed the rope and slashed it. He dropped the horsehair rope and slid the knife away. He stepped quietly behind the horses, and pulled the Dragoon. "Go on, git!" he roared, then fired the two shots remaining in the Colt into the ground right behind one pony's rump.

The horses bolted, whinnying and snorting.

Calhoun sighed and began reloading the pistol. When the job was done and the revolver nestled in the plain leather holster, Calhoun reached up and felt his left ear. His hand came away spotted with blood, but he didn't figure it was too bad.

He picked up his rifle, checked it swiftly, and then started heading toward where he could see into the gully. He moved cautiously, though not too slowly. He thought—perhaps hoped was the better word— that the Apaches were more interested in getting their horses back than they were in killing him.

He came up on one of the few decent-size trees in the area, and stopped behind it. He held a commanding view of the countryside. The last of the Apache horses were just charging up the slope opposite him. He caught glimpses of two Apaches over there moving to head the ponies off.

Calhoun wanted to check out the Apaches' new position, if they had any. But his original quarry— the bandits and the woman—were gone. By the cloud of dust, he could tell they were heading out of the canyon the way he had come in, and they must be pushing the mules hard.

"Dammit all," Calhoun snarled. He turned and ran, heading for his horse. He was none too quick, though, considering he had reopened the wound, which was seeping blood, his wrenched ankle, from where he had turned it, and all the deadly and stealthy exertions he had been though in the past several hours.

After a few yards, he slowed to a walk. Getting there five minutes sooner would not help him catch the bandits any faster. Besides, he needed to conserve what strength and reserves he had left for what was to come. He didn't think capturing or killing the bandits was going to be too easy.

There also was still a good chance that he might

have to contend with the Apaches again. They would not be in good spirits after the whipping he had just given them, and whether or not they knew he was involved, if they found him, they would try to make short work of him. It would be sufficient for them that he was an Anglo.

He hobbled on, moving as fast as he dared considering his small injuries and his desire to build up his considerable reserves. He also was alert to the possible coming of Apaches. None showed his face, though, and Calhoun was at least a little thankful for that.

As he walked, he heard the faint rumble of wagons and horses. It quickly faded. A red-tailed hawk whistled piercingly high overhead.

He estimated it was more than twenty minutes before he reached his horse and mule, still tucked away in the crack in the cliff wall. The horse seemed grateful to see him, shaking its full white mane and swishing the heavy white-haired tail. Calhoun patted the beast on the head. "Damn fool animal," he said to it quietly. "If only you knew about me and horses."

He slid the Henry into the saddle scabbard and walked the two animals out into the shallow canyon. There he pulled himself wearily onto the horse's back. He took the rope to the mule in hand and rode on out. The sun was sinking down behind the peaks of the Patagonia Mountains, creating a sky of streaked pink, orange, and red.

The display of God's palette did nothing to improve Calhoun's sour spirits. He scowled, knowing he was not likely to catch the bandits before darkness came. Calhoun kicked the sorrel a little, urging the animal into a trot that jarred his insides with each pace.

Back in the wide valley between the Canelo Hills and the Patagonia Mountains, he stopped and scanned the horizon. He saw a cloud of dust to the southwest, which made sense to him. The bandits were headed to Mexico, but were also getting closer to the Patagonias should the Apaches show up again. Having seen those mountains from a distance, Calhoun felt sure they would provide a more defensible stronghold than the hills had.

Calhoun moved in that direction, trotting at first, but then slowing to a walk as the shadows lengthened. He figured that sooner or later, the bandits would pull into the mountains to spend the night. Calhoun did not want to pass them.

When the dusk had deepened to cover most of the valley, Calhoun stopped. He had found a clump of Emory oaks and figured it was as likely as anyplace else he might find. He tied the animals and unloaded the mule. After that, he unsaddled the sorrel and spent some time rubbing the horse down. The horse had performed well despite the intensity of the day's heat, which had not dissipated any yet, and so deserved to be taken care of.

By the time he finished that, it was fully dark. He stumbled around until he found wood for a fire. He piled rocks against a small boulder, forming a horseshoe with the opening toward the mountains. He built his small fire in it, certain that no one would be able to see the flames.

As his supper cooked, he went to his supplies and pulled out one of the two bottles of whiskey he had brought with him. He rolled a cigarette, lit it, and then uncorked the bottle.

He ate, and then tossed his utensils aside. He had another cigarette and a few more swigs of whiskey before stretching out atop his bedroll.

CHAPTER

* 23 *

Calhoun picked up the trail in the morning, still heading southwest. He saw no dust on the horizon, but did not think that unusual. He figured Sepulveda's men knew where they were, and had traveled through much, if not most, of the night.

Calhoun kept an eye out behind him, too, for Apaches. He was glad he was in this valley, where no one could sneak up on him. He knew an attack could come from the mountains to his right, but they were still half a mile or so to the west. The Indians, or anyone else, would have to cover a fair piece of open ground before they could get to him. Of course, since he was out in that open ground, there was no place he could make a stand should the Apaches, or the bandits, come at him hard.

The day was the same as ever—hot. The sun blazed down in bright yellow malevolence. Not a cloud broke the staggeringly brilliant blue of the sky, offering no hope of even momentary relief. He was sweating buckets before he was a half-hour from camp.

Calhoun kept his pace deliberately slow. He wanted to catch the bandits more than anything right now, but killing his horse in the heat would not accomplish anything. He wondered if the reason he saw no dust was because the bandits had enough sense to hole up in a copse or in a cave up in the Patagonias or maybe some shaded canyon in the mountains.

The bandits had passed this way for sure, Calhoun knew, since the tracks were easy enough to read in the harsh, blistering glare of the sun. How long ago, though, he could not tell.

About noon, judging by the angle of the omnipresent sun, he stopped and slid off the horse. He loosened the saddle, allowing the sorrel to breathe. He gulped from his canteen and then filled his frying pan with water, since his hat was filled with holes. He held the pan for the horse to drink from. He repeated the process for the mule. It left him with precious little water in his canteen.

A light breeze sprang up while he stood there, but it offered him no relief. All it did was force the heat of the day to tear at his face rather than brush it. The breeze also picked up dust particles, which blasted his face with minuscule pellets.

He finally tightened the saddle and climbed aboard the horse, pressing on. As the time passed, Calhoun thought he could feel his tongue swelling from thirst. His mouth was dry and seemed sticky.

For the most part, he rode with his eyes closed against the brittle, merciless glare of the sun, opening them only occasionally to check the bleak, fried landscape around him. It never seemed to change, and he began to think after a while that he was not actually going anywhere. That the sorrel was walking in place somehow. Mirages cropped up from time to time, annoying Calhoun with their false promises.

About four hours after he had first stopped, he saw the horse's ears perk up. He looked behind and saw that the mule seemed more attentive. The pack animal's ears also were cocked, and the big snout probed the air. *It must mean there's water nearby,* Calhoun was sure. He shrugged and let the horse pick up the pace a little bit.

Suddenly the horse broke into a gallop, nostrils flared, ears cocked forward. The mule followed eagerly. Calhoun did not slow the animals.

A few minutes later they came on a wide, muddy track that Calhoun figured was a creek or river when there was real water available. The sorrel found a puddle and dipped his muzzle into it and drank greedily.

Calhoun dismounted , boots sinking a little into the mushy mud. There was no real flow of water, but there were trickles here and there, and occasional puddles. He led the mule to one of the puddles and let it drink.

While the animals drank, Calhoun walked to one of the trickles. Since it was running, however slightly, it would not be as stagnant as the puddles. He knelt in the soft black mud and scooped water into his mouth with a cupped hand.

It took a while for the man and two animals to get their fill, but at last they were sated. Calhoun got his canteen and managed to jam it far enough into the mud that the trickle ran right over the mouth. He left it there to fill, while he loosened the horse's saddle.

He squished through the mud to another puddle and knelt beside it. Pulling the sweat-soaked bandanna from his pocket, he soaked it in the puddle, then squeezed the water out over his hair. He repeated it several times before taking the sopping cloth and running it over his face and neck.

When he stood and slapped his hat back on, he felt considerably refreshed. With slightly renewed spirits, he retrieved his full canteen and capped it. He hung it from the saddle horn and then tightened the cinch on his fancy, single-rig saddle. Grabbing the rope to the mule, he pulled himself onto the sorrel and moved on.

Calhoun figured he must be in Mexico by now, or damn close to it. The countryside was as desolate as ever. It was, Calhoun decided, a land fit only for Apaches and bandits.

Within half a mile of the stream, the wagon tracks abruptly turned right. Calhoun stopped the horse and sat a few minutes, eyes moving across the barrenness. He saw nothing other than a hawk, or maybe an eagle, soaring over the mountains. There was no dust to be seen, no glint of sunlight on a rifle barrel. Nor was anything heard except the screech of the raptor, the hot rustle of the breeze, and the creaking of his saddle leather.

It was eerie, as if he were the only man left on earth. It was as if God had simply wiped the earth, or at least this part of it, clean of all things living, having missed Calhoun and that bird in the doing.

It didn't so much unnerve Calhoun as make him think he was hallucinating. He half expected to wake up in Lucille's bed back in Tubac, to see her plain, strong, loving face next to him, to feel her long, lean lines pressed against him.

He blinked several times, and knew that this was real; that the other was just the dream. He rolled a cigarette as he continued checking out the land. He cupped the match against the breeze and lit the cigarette, then looked behind him. There was nothing there, either, except this harsh, bitter land stretching on to infinity.

Calhoun shook his head at it all. He had been across the wide expanse of the Great Plains more times than he could count. That was a wide, empty land, but there was always something living to be seen there—buffalo or antelope or deer, wagons passing by the score, birds, rattlesnakes, rabbits, coyotes, and wolves, even bears of a time. Out here, there was nothing except that one bird of prey. It was even too hot for the scorpions and big diamondback rattlers that he knew were out here.

He crushed out the butt of his cigarette on the callused interdigital pads, where the fingers met the palm of his left hand, and scattered the remainder of the butt to the wind. The sense of urgency had renewed itself in his heart with a vengeance. He kicked the horse.

The track began winding upward almost immediately. There was not really a trail. It was simply that the men with the wagons had found the easiest way around the rocks, sage, and cactus and had followed it. There were more shadows here, since the sun was slipping behind the mountains he was entering. He found it hard to judge how much light he had left.

He would like to at least locate the bandits before darkness came, but he could not risk abusing the horse to do so. Besides, the track he was following had enough twists and turns and switchbacks that he might run into the bandits at any moment. That would be interesting, he figured.

Calhoun also knew that it could be easy for the bandits to pick him out—and shoot him down—long before he got to their camp, if they were vigilant enough. After the bandits' escapade with the Apaches, Calhoun suspected the Mexicans would be tense and extra cautious. They would almost assuredly place guards on whatever camp they had.

Of course, it was possible that they were not going to camp anywhere near here. From talking with people in Tubac, Calhoun had gotten an idea of the land in these parts. He knew the Patagonia Mountains were not all that big, although the major peak was fairly tall. It shouldn't take much to get through them and into the large valley through which the Santa Cruz River ran straight from Tubac. Turning south, one would be at Nogales, the place of the walnut grove, with a short ride.

It grew harder to read the trail as the vegetation gave way to more places of barren rock. Calhoun pressed on the same "trail," however, despite passing numerous holes into the mountain. None of those places, though, would be able to shelter three wagons, almost twenty people, and more than two dozen horses.

Two hours later, though, he lost the track. He stopped and turned halfway around in the saddle. He had come across more than three quarters of a mile of rock, where no track could be seen in the best case. Somewhere in that stretch, they must have turned off.

Calhoun went over the terrain in his mind. There were two or three places they might have gone. None had struck him as likely places to take wagons, but they must have taken one of them. He turned the horse and mule around and rode back.

When he came on the first one from the west, he edged the horse's nose into the canyon mouth. It became evident within minutes that this canyon, which snaked in rugged, rocky splendor to the north, would never open far enough to allow the wagons to be brought in. It was the same with the next, which also made a thin, jagged foray to the north.

As Calhoun approached the third one —this one opening southward—he felt a surge of excitement. It had to be this one, he told himself silently. It just had to be.

He dismounted and tied the horse and mule to a chunk of rock. On foot, he carefully moved into the crack in the mountain's face. Just past the rock entryway, the canyon opened widely. Calhoun stopped immediately, flattened against the rock, and looked around. He was sure no one could have seen him, unless they were looking through a spyglass at the very moment he moved one foot out into the canyon and then jerked it back.

He could see wagon tracks leading into the

canyon in the few places where there was enough soil to take an impression. The bottom of the canyon, which snaked southwest after a hard turn about fifty yards in, was already in heavy shadow. Before long it would be completely dark. Calhoun could see no reason to rush in. There was still enough light that he could easily be spotted. If worse came to worst, he figured, he could make his way into the canyon at night. He would etch enough of the canyon's features into his mind to be able to get a decent distance in and hole up until he could learn more.

Twenty minutes later he came straight up, alert, when he spotted a glimmer of something metallic reflected in the sun. It had come from the southeastern wall, about halfway up. Calhoun fixed the spot in his mind.

He moved back toward the entrance of the canyon a little and crossed to the other side of the rock wall. Then he slid forward again, wanting to check the opposite wall of the canyon to see if a guard was posted there, too. He didn't think he'd be able to see much, seeing as how the western wall was deep in shadow now. He found out it didn't really matter that he couldn't see. The wall for most of the length Calhoun could see was too sheer to allow a guard.

Calhoun swung back to where he was to begin with. Twice more before the canyon went dark forty minutes later he saw the faint glint of sun on metal, the last time some distance lower than the first. As Calhoun walked back to get the horse and mule, he knew the guard was heading back toward the camp since he would not be able to see anything in the dark. Calhoun also knew that the outlaws would have a guard posted somewhere outside the camp. He would have to find that man and remove him before he could start his assault on the bandit camp.

As he moved into the canyon, on foot, leading the horse and mule, he could see several campfires off in the distance. He almost smiled as his blood raced with excitement. He worked his way down into the canyon, moving carefully. Having a map in his mind helped, but it was not perfect, nor could it account for every rock and stone.

As he reached the floor of the canyon, he moved straight ahead. Three hundred yards in, he veered left. He had spotted a patch of mesquite that should shelter the animals. There was some grass around and through the copse, offering the animals something to graze on.

After tying the animals to branches, he pulled a hard leather pouch from his saddlebags. Into it he put the two extra loaded cylinders he kept for the Dragoons. He also made sure he had enough paper cartridges in the belt pouch he already wore for the pistols, and for the shotgun.

He hung the second pouch on his gun belt. Then Calhoun pulled out the ten-gauge double-barrel Greener shotgun.

CHAPTER

* 24 *

Calhoun crept through the trees and brush that lined the bottom of the canyon. Enough moonlight filtered through the foliage to give him a little feeble light. He appreciated that, though at the same time he knew it would allow a guard to see a little, too.

The guard worried him more than a little. Not that he was afraid of him, or of any other man. However, the guard most likely knew this land, and could sit tight, while Calhoun would have to be on the move. More important, though, the guard would be alert. Normally, in a secluded canyon like this, miles from anywhere, the bandits could be expected to be rather lax. After the Apache raid, though, the guard would be tense and wary. It would make Calhoun's job a lot harder.

Calhoun didn't let that overly worry him, though. The guard would have to be found and dispatched. That was all there was to it. Though Calhoun wanted to do it silently, if possible, he figured that if noise erupted, the others would put it down to another Apache attack.

Once the guard was taken care of, he could figure out how to get into the camp and what he would do when he got there. There could be no way he could make a plan now, if ever, for this job, so worrying about it was a waste of time. And Calhoun was not one to waste time on such things.

Occasionally, Calhoun could catch the twinkling of the fires ahead, through the brush and trees. It gave him a bearing to fix on in the often inky darkness of the canyon.

As he drew nearer—he estimated a hundred yards or so—to the camp, he slowed his pace. Soon after, he began stopping every few feet to listen and scan the blackness. He could hear sounds from the camp now, mostly men talking and laughing. It began to sound almost like the men were celebrating. Calhoun supposed they were feeling good about escaping the Apaches. That and the fact that they had all those women there with them would be as good an excuse as any for whooping it up some.

That could work in Calhoun's favor, he knew, especially if they had some whiskey with them. It would be a hell of a lot easier to invade a camp of men who were snoring in drunken slumber. While Calhoun did not fear dying, he did not want to get killed and leave the dozen women in the bandits' clutches. Yet going against seven battle-hardened bandits by himself would be a good way of doing just that.

Calhoun stopped once more and listened. Just as he was about to step off again, he heard a stifled sneeze. Calhoun froze, trying not even to breathe. He was beginning to think that the sound would never come again, that perhaps he had even imagined it, when it was repeated, this time followed by a muffled, annoyed, "Jesus Cristos."

Calhoun nodded to himself, smiling viciously in the darkness. He had the man pegged now. Taking each step as if he were walking on burning coals, he moved basically toward where the guard was. But not directly. He angled out a little, wanting to come up from the man's side or back.

It seemed to take forever, but eventually Calhoun sensed, more than felt, that he was near the man. Then he heard two voices speaking softly in Spanish. He froze, waiting. It would, he thought, be easy to kill both men now, while they were changing guards, thus meaning he would have fewer to face when he got to the camp. Then he decided that if he did that, the bandits still in the camp would become suspicious when the first guard did not return within a few minutes. That would put them on alert. He decided to wait, though he did edge up a little closer.

When he heard one man moving quietly off, Calhoun carefully rested the shotgun against the trunk of a small, broad live oak, then moved on again, one careful step after the other. He stopped when he was close enough to reach out and touch the bandit's back.

The man was hard to see in the darkness, but the silvery light that spread feebly over the canyon highlighted him sufficiently, especially when he moved his head, and the large sombrero went with it. He was a big man, though not all that tall. His back was broad, hinting that he was carrying around a considerable amount of excess weight.

Calhoun slid out the big Bowie and took two swift steps forward.

The guard sensed the danger he was in and made a move as if to turn. Before he could, though, Calhoun shoved the Bowie knife to the hilt into the man's back.

Calhoun's left hand snapped out and grabbed the back of the guard's sweat-soaked shirt. By dint of sheer strength, he kept the guard from crashing to the ground. Then he eased the man down, pulled out the knife, and wiped it off on the back of the Mexican's shirt.

As he slipped the Bowie back into the sheath dangling under his left arm, Calhoun looked around, and listened intently. Nothing had changed in the bandit camp, as far as he could tell. He nodded, spun, and walked swiftly and silently to where his shotgun was. He picked it up and headed toward the camp.

Though he was moving more quickly now, he was still wary. He knew that just because he had killed one guard did not mean there weren't others posted. He had the sudden, chilling thought that perhaps the bandits had met others of their kind here. That would explain the many raids in the area, he figured. Two or three bands of half a dozen or so men each, riding and raiding, and then meeting here to pool the booty before riding into Mexico. Or maybe this was Mexico, and so they felt safer, thinking that the angry *Americanos* wouldn't or couldn't chase them here.

Then he shook off the feeling. This was no band

of a couple dozen bandits meeting for the first time in weeks. He was just a little jumpy. That was unusual for him, but he put it down to the fact that no one had mattered to him in a long time, and he was worried about rescuing Lucille. That and the fact that he had seen an owl on his way into the canyon.

He neared the camp slowly. He stopped behind a large, bushy chuparosa and surveyed what he could of the bandits' camp. The four fires threw a fair amount of light, and he could see pretty well.

The camp was in a small meadow surrounded by small oaks, mesquites, paloverdes, even some ironwood. To the far right, running in a ragged diagonal, was a thin trickle of a stream. Calhoun supposed it would be dry more often than not during the summer. To his right was one of the wagons, and another was partway around the "circle" beyond. Calhoun could see women there. He wasn't sure all the women were there, but certainly the majority. The third wagon was to his left. A fire burned in front of each wagon, with the fourth toward the back of the camp.

Along the far side and most of the left side were the horses, and the mules used for the wagons. Ropes were tied between several trees, and the horses were tied to the ropes, front and back, facing each other.

Five bandits were gathered around the fourth fire, which left one unaccounted for. Calhoun did not move, except for rotating his head slowly, trying to spot the other bandit. Doing so became considerably easier when he heard an annoyed, frightened squeal from near the wagon to his right.

Calhoun slipped off through the trees and brush, heading toward the wagon. He stopped and squatted behind a short yucca. With the firelight behind the wagon, he could see the bandit coupling with an unwilling partner. Calhoun shook his head in annoyance. He never could understand how a man could force himself on a woman like that. It wasn't very manly, to his way of thinking, and couldn't be very pleasurable. Besides, there were too many willing women around.

There was nothing Calhoun could do to help the woman now, short of shooting the bandit, which he considered for a moment. Then he discarded the idea. He still didn't fully know what he faced here, and he had no way of killing all the bandits before they hit the brush. Trying to track down five bandits in a dark canyon filled with brush and trees could easily be fatal.

He spun silently and moved off, circling around the back side of the wagon and following the stream. There was water in it, but not much. Mostly it was a two-foot-wide mud slick. He tried to stay out of the mud, not because of any sense of fastidiousness but because he did not want the sucking mud to give him away.

Calhoun stopped behind a mesquite and looked over the women. He spotted Señorita Luna, the chubby young woman who had been accosted by Wilson in Juan Sosa's store that first time Calhoun had gone in there.

He tried not to let his hopes rise, but they did. And crashed just as quickly when he did not spot

Lucille among the women. Unless she was somewhere else in the camp—and he doubted that very much—he figured she must be dead.

Trying not to let his heartsickness, or his rage, get the better of him, he completely circled the camp, stopping periodically to look things over. One time he halted among the horses, standing there and looking straight at the men around the fire, his hate building slowly in his chest.

As far as they were dressed, all the bandits looked pretty much the same as far as Calhoun could see. All wore short, tight jackets of buckskin, wool pants that seemed to be slightly flared at the bottom, and sombreros, all of the same basic, indistinguishable mousy grayish-brown color. Some were taller than others, he supposed, and it was obvious that some were heavy and some were thin. Of the three he could see the faces of, one had a small, scrubby goatee, one had a thin mustache and a half moon scar on his left cheekbone, and the other was clean-shaven and had a large gap where several teeth used to be. They generated no sympathy in his heart.

He completed the circuit and stopped behind the chuparosa where he had first stopped after killing the guard. He checked the moon, and figured it had been four hours since he had left the canyon mouth. He estimated that he had about four more hours before light. Plenty of time. He was only a little surprised to see that everyone was still awake. He figured the women were too frightened to sleep, especially since the men were using them with at least minimum frequency; and the men were celebrating.

Calhoun watched as one of the bandits rose and said something in a low, raspy voice. The bandits all laughed, and the one walked toward the wagon where the women were gathered. He grabbed one by the shoulder and started hauling her toward the other wagon, tossing his sombrero aside as he did. Calhoun moved in that direction, too.

The bandit shoved the woman under the wagon, and started to crawl under it after her, loosening his pants as he did. He was looking at the woman, a leer on his face. His look changed to one of surprise as he heard a gun being cocked. He glanced up and looked down the muzzle of a shotgun less than a foot from his face.

"I ain't fond of alertin' your pals that I'm here," Calhoun whispered. "But you so much as belch and you'll not be around to worry about it. You got that, *amigo*?"

The thin, high-cheekboned head went up and down once. The man's tongue eased out and circled his lips. He could see the hard face of the man squatting behind the shotgun.

"Come on out this way and stand. Easy."

Once again the head bobbed. That was his only movement, though. He was not about to go anywhere with that shotgun stuck in his face.

"Ma'am," Calhoun said, "just wait here till I come back. Understand?"

"Yes," the woman said in a creaky voice.

"All right, *amigo*," Calhoun said to the bandit. "Move." He moved back a little. When the bandit was partway out, Calhoun stood. The shotgun followed the man as he, too, rose. "Lace your hands behind your head, boy."

When the bandit had done so, Calhoun waved the shotgun toward the brush. The bandit began walking there.

Manuel Melendrez was worried. He had thought as he crawled out from under the wagon that perhaps he was more impressed with this man than he should have been simply because the shotgun made the man fierce. But as he stood and looked into those cold, deadly eyes, he knew his initial impression of fear at Calhoun was not false.

As he walked, Melendrez became certain that he would die, and soon. He wondered what he might do to prevent that. He could not shout for help, since that would mean instant death. About all he could hope for was to perhaps duck behind a tree, yank out his pistol, and blast this gringo bastard. Even if he died then, he would take the *loco Americano* with him.

He was still considering that when Calhoun ordered him to stop. He did, eyes flicking left and right, looking for a place to duck to. There wasn't much, except a mesquite a few yards to his left. It might have to do.

On the other hand, he thought, maybe the man wasn't going to kill him. He would not want to make too much noise. Perhaps this gringo simply wanted to tie him up and try to rescue the women.

He was still thinking such hopeful thoughts when Calhoun, who had uncocked his shotgun and gently placed it on the ground, grabbed Melendrez around the mouth from behind. Before Melendrez could react, Calhoun's sharp Bowie had opened his throat.

CHAPTER

✷ 25 ✷

Calhoun eased Melendrez's body down, wiped the blade off on the man's jacket, and put the knife away. Then he turned, picked up his shotgun, and moved swiftly back to the wagon where he had left the woman. He knelt there and whispered, "Slide out this way, ma'am."

The woman jerked her head around in fear, then relaxed ever so slightly when she saw it was not one of the bandits. She squiggled until she was out from under the wagon. Calhoun helped her up. She was shorter than he had expected, and had a plump, full figure. Her long black hair hung loose, framing her round little face and lying heavily on her shoulders.

"What's your name, ma'am?" he asked in a whisper.

"Marisol Zbarra," the woman answered in kind.

Calhoun nodded. "Where's Lucille?" he asked with a note of urgency in his voice.

"Who?"

"Señora Viejo."

"She is not with us, señor," Marisol said. She seemed surprised.

"What?" Calhoun hissed. He was more shocked at Marisol's answer than Marisol had been at his question.

"She is not with us, señor," Marisol repeated.

Calhoun pulled the woman a little away from the wagon, toward the brush. "Where is she then?" he asked. His voice was still soft, so as not to be heard, but there was unmistakable worry in the tones.

"I don't know, señor," Marisol said. She was frightened. First she had been forced to go along with the bandits and made to suffer all sorts of indignities. Now she had this wild-eyed gringo staring at her and asking her strange questions.

"These bastards kill her somewhere along the trail?"

"Señora Viejo was not with us." Marisol was confused as well as frightened.

"Never?"

"No, señor."

"Damn," Calhoun breathed. He stood there, a plethora of thoughts tumbling around in his brain. It took but a few moments before the thoughts began to coalesce into something workable. It could be only one thing, he realized: Goodykoontz had lied to him. The real question now was, Why?

He sighed. There would be no answer to that until he got back to Tubac. Now, at least, he had a reason to return to Tubac, and fast. First he had to get the women away from the bandits and remove the outlaws.

Now that he had a purpose, he was filled with a desire to move fast. "All right, señora," he said. "Which . . ."

"It is señorita."

"Sorry . . . señorita. Which one is Sepulveda?"

"The one with the thin mustache, and the half-moon scar on his cheek." She pointed shyly to her own prominent left cheekbone.

Calhoun nodded. "I want you to get back to the other women," he said. "Tell 'em someone's here to help 'em. Then you're all to wait there."

"For what?"

"Till you're free." It was, for Calhoun, a simple statement of fact.

Señorita Zbarra nodded, hope beginning to flicker in her breast. "But what if one of those men comes . . . for . . . one of us?" Her voice quavered.

"He'll die sooner rather than later," Calhoun said flatly.

Señorita Zbarra nodded, her fear somewhat mitigated by the bluntness of Calhoun's statement. She wasn't sure why she was so trusting in this man, except perhaps that he had already saved her from one of the *bandidos*. She turned and walked hastily, trying not to draw any attention to herself, back to the wagon where the other women were.

She realized as she arrived there that she did not even know her savior's name. Shrugging that lack of knowledge off, she quickly and excitedly began whispering to her companions.

"What does he look like?" Señorita Luna asked. She began to suspect something.

Señorita Zbarra described Calhoun.

Señorita Luna nodded. *"Sí, sí,"* she said in a vigorous whisper. She swiftly explained how Calhoun had helped her in Sosa's store.

All the women suddenly felt much better.

* * *

Calhoun had slipped back into the brush and made his way as quickly as he dared around the camp toward where the men were still gathered around the fire. As he moved, he kept flicking glances into the camp, wanting to make sure that none of the other bandits decided to have a woman. He hoped not, since that would force his hand prematurely, though he would not hesitate if it came to that.

Calhoun moved up among the horses, moving slowly, carefully, not wanting to startle the animals. It had been less than five minutes since the one bandit had pulled Señorita Zbarra away from her friends.

He stood there watching the men as they laughed. There was a jug present, and the men were passing it around, but none of the bandits seemed drunk. One laughed sickeningly, and craned his head toward the wagon. He called out something in Spanish, and then laughed again.

Someone else spoke in Spanish and they all laughed some more. Calhoun was a little surprised, but he supposed from where they were sitting, they could not really see under the wagon across the dark camp.

During another burst of the lecherous laughter, Calhoun cocked the shotgun. He drew in a deep breath and let it out slowly. As he stepped out into the open, a cruel smile began to spread across his face.

Before he had taken four steps beyond the horses, Calhoun fired both barrels of the shotgun. Two bandits died, their backs shredded by buckshot.

By the time the three others began to react, Calhoun had one of his Dragoons out. He fired smoothly, evenly, as he walked. Two more of the bandits—including Sepulveda—died, bullets in their chests. Calhoun turned toward the last, ready to blast that bandit into oblivion, too.

Then he hesitated. He did so not out of any fear or compassion, but practicality. He had wanted to keep Sepulveda alive in the hopes that the bandit leader could tell him something, perhaps explain what had happened in Tubac, possibly something about Lucille. Since he considered Sepulveda too dangerous and had blasted him, perhaps this other bandit would do.

The hesitation allowed the bandit to get his pistol out, though he was half lying down. The man's dark face was twisted up in an angry snarl as he jerked the pistol's hammer back with his thumb.

Calhoun fired the last two shots in the Dragoon. One ball shattered the bandit's gun wrist, the other the humerus of the same arm. The man dropped his pistol, having no choice about it. The jerk caused by Calhoun's bullet plowing into his wrist had made the pistol go off, however. The bullet screamed away harmlessly into the night.

Calhoun dropped the Dragoon into the holster and pulled the other one. He moved toward the bandit, who had rolled onto his stomach and was trying to grab his fallen revolver with his left hand. Calhoun stepped on the man's good arm. "Y'all don't need that, pal," he said quietly.

The bandit looked up over his shoulder. His face displayed no sign of pain, though there was plenty of hate evident.

Calhoun moved his foot. "Roll over on your back."

The Mexican could see no reason to refuse. That, he figured, would bring instant death. While he was alive, there was some hope of killing this gringo bastard. He did as he was told.

"*¿Cómo se llama?*" Calhoun asked. "What's your name?"

The man said nothing.

"His name's Francisco Azevedo. He is—was—Sepulveda's main lieutenant."

Calhoun turned and saw Señorita Luna standing there bravely. The other women hung back, but had left their huddled haven near the wagon. Calhoun nodded at Señorita Luna and turned back to look at Azevedo. "Tell me about Tubac," he ordered.

"*No habla Inglés.*"

Calhoun stomped on Azevedo's smashed wrist with his heel. Azevedo's eyes rolled up into his head, and he sucked in air. When he had calmed back down again, and glared hatefully at Calhoun, the saddle tramp said, "Tell me about Tubac."

"What do you want to know?" His voice was heavily accented.

"Who's givin' you information about when to raid there?"

Azevedo glared at Calhoun in annoyance. "How do you know that?" he asked, his accented words short and sharp.

"I'm mighty goddamn short on patience, boy," Calhoun rasped.

Azevedo believed him. Francisco Azevedo was not afraid of dying, but he did not want to be stomped to death, or die some lingering, pain-filled death. "You won't believe me," he said.

"Tell me anyway."

Azevedo licked his lips. "Señor Goodykoontz." His accent mangled the name, but it was still understandable.

Calhoun nodded. He was not surprised. He supposed he had suspected it since Señorita Zbarra told him that Lucille was not with the women here, and never had been. Now he knew why Goodykoontz had lied to him. "How'd he work it?"

Azevedo shrugged, then regretted it as pain raced through his arm. When the agony settled down to a bearable level, he said, "He would get word to us when to raid the town. Other places, too."

"He tell you what to take?"

"*Sí*. Sometimes. Other times, he told us to do what we wanted, but to leave certain places alone."

"Why ain't the Army come after you?"

"The gringo soldiers are *cobarde*—chicken-hearted."

"That's a pile of shit," Calhoun said without conviction. After having met Major Heydrich, he had some doubts about the Army's efficiency.

Azevedo shrugged. How was he, a simple Mexican

bandit, to know what motivated the *Americanos?*

Calhoun finally asked the question that had been on his tongue all along, but that he had been loathe to ask for fear of the answer: "Where is Lucille?"

"Who?"

Calhoun's eyes flared hotly, but he cooled himself right away. The bandit could not be expected to know Lucille's first name. "Señora Viejo."

"Ah, the gringa." He shrugged.

"Goodykoontz said you kidnapped her along with all these others." Calhoun's heart was sinking.

"We did not take the gringa."

"Señor Calhoun?" Señorita Luna said tentatively. When he faced her, she said, "Maybe I can help." Her voice was squeaky with fear and worry.

Calhoun nodded, curious.

"Several days before these . . . these animals . . . carried me and the others away, I saw Señor Perlmutter and Señor Goodykoontz going into the señora's house." Señorita Luna stopped, afraid to continue.

Calhoun nodded, rage flooding through him.

"Maybe Señor Fat wanted to enjoy the señora, and she didn't live under the weight," Azevedo said. "Maybe he needed his . . . assistant"—he snickered in derision—"to help him with the gringa." He tried to laugh, but it hurt too much, so he choked it off quickly.

Calhoun was almost blinded by the rage that welled up inside him, and he managed to control it only with a supreme effort.

"It wouldn't be the first time such a thing has happened, señor," Azevedo said flatly.

Calhoun's thoughts were jumbled, but he began

to sort things out quickly. Goodykoontz must have killed Lucille when he was through with her, and then sent Calhoun on this wild-goose chase. Still, the question of why remained. Not that it mattered much now. The evidence was overwhelming that Lucille was dead, and that Goodykoontz was responsible, either directly or indirectly.

"She wasn't much to look at," Azevedo added, "but what the hell, Señor Lard couldn't be too choosy. Maybe she even enjoyed the idea. Goodykoontz was such a big man . . ." Azevedo cackled.

The rage Calhoun had felt before was nothing to the eruption of fury at both Azevedo's words and the sudden certainty that Lucille was dead. His eyes narrowed, and he thumbed back the Dragoon's hammer. He took a step forward and fired three times. The three bullets turned Azevedo's face into a bloody mush.

Behind him, Señorita Luna turned pale, Señorita Zbarra got sick, and another woman fainted.

CHAPTER

* 26 *

"**Y**ou *mujers*—women—best get some rest," Calhoun said. "I aim to be on the trail come first light." He actually was of a notion to go get his flaxen sorrel and ride out right now. A desire to get to Tubac and carve up Madison Goodykoontz flamed deeply inside of him. He had the women to think of now, however. He could not just let them try to make their way back to Tubac by themselves.

The women drifted off toward the wagon where they had been before. They did not know where else to go, and they were not about to stand there amid the blood and bodies.

Calhoun hastily cleaned and reloaded his pistols, and then began moving around the camp, checking things. First he made sure all the bandits were dead; then he began taking stock of what they had that was usable. As he walked, his stomach growled from hunger, and he wished he had not told the women to go to sleep yet. He wished now that he had asked one or two of them to make him some food.

He looked almost wistfully toward the women, and saw with a note of surprise that they were not settling in to sleep. Instead, they were sitting there talking excitedly. Calhoun realized after a moment that it made sense. They had had an extremely traumatic few days, culminating in a night of terror, violence, and salvation. They would need to talk.

Calhoun let them be. He would make himself something to eat after a while. He had work to do, and he knew he would not be able to sleep just yet anyway. Not after the excitement of the night.

The wagons were full of goods from Tubac, though most were of little use to Calhoun or the women. He did find sufficient stores of food and ammunition, as well as two full water barrels lashed to the side of a wagon. Another problem he faced was what to do with the women and the wagons. He did not want to bring the wagons with him, since they would slow him down considerably. In addition, he could not drive all three, and he was fairly certain that none of the women knew how to handle a mule team.

He pushed the thought from his mind. There would be time for worrying about that later. He headed toward the sitting women, who turned to face him as they became aware of his approach.

"I aim to get my horse, which I left tied up near the canyon mouth," he announced. "I'll be back directly."

Some of the women looked frightened, which Calhoun could understand in them. They had been through a lot lately. "All the bandits are dead," he said quietly. "You don't have to worry about them."

"But what about the Apaches?" one asked in a quavering voice.

Calhoun shrugged. "Never can tell with them, I guess." He paused, stroking the stubble on his chin. "But I figure that if they was around, they would've done something by now." It was the best he could offer them.

He spun and walked off, rejecting the thought of taking a torch. If there were Apaches around, he didn't need to make a target of himself. He moved swiftly, though cautiously, following the vague trail the bandits had used coming in. It did not take long to get the horse and mule.

He rode back into the camp, unsaddled the horse and unloaded the mule. After rubbing the horse down, he got two feed bags and filled them with grain he had found among the bandits' stores. As he was hanging one feed bag over the horse's head, Señorita Luna approached.

"May I speak with you, señor?" she asked in a soft, melodious voice. She seemed nervous, or maybe embarrassed.

"Of course."

"You would like to get back to Tubac quickly, yes?"

Calhoun grunted an acknowledgment as he finished his chore and then reached for the other feed bag.

"So would we, Señor Calhoun." Señorita Luna waited, hardly daring to breathe, hoping she had not overstepped her bounds.

"I can understand that, señorita," Calhoun said, turning to look at her as the mule began munching.

"We would like to leave now, señor."

"It ain't gonna be easy." He felt more than a little foolish saying it, but felt he had to give them some warning.

"It has not been easy since we were taken from Tubac, señor," Señorita Luna said quietly.

Calhoun nodded, accepting the acknowledgment of his warning. "Any of you know how to ride astride?" he asked.

Señorita Luna shook her head. "Most of us don't even know how to ride sidesaddle. Can't you take us in one of the wagons?"

"I don't think it'd be wise for me to be drivin' a wagon. It'd be safer was I to ride and keep an eye on things. Just 'cause there ain't no Apaches here now don't mean there ain't none out there along the trail somewhere."

They were silent a moment, thinking. Suddenly Señorita Luna brightened. "Inez knows how to drive a wagon!" she said breathlessly.

"Who?"

"Inez Lugo. Her father, Hector, runs a small freighting company. She learned to drive his wagons."

"She be willin' to drive a wagon with the rest of you women in it?"

"*Sí !*"

Calhoun nodded slowly, more acknowledging to himself that the plan might work rather than giving his permission. She understood and waited. "All right," he said finally. "But there's chores to be done before we ride."

"We will do them," Señorita Luna said without hesitation.

"*Bueno.* First, I need one of you to cook me food, and a big pot of coffee, *comprendes?*" He didn't wait for an answer. "And I'll need help unloadin' one of the wagons if we want to make any speed. After I've eaten, I'll hitch up the mules. We ought to be on the trail in an hour."

Señorita Luna nodded. "What about the other wagons? And all the things that were taken from Tubac?"

"Ain't nothing in there I want or need," Calhoun said with a shrug.

"I suppose the people of Tubac can live without all those things," Señorita Luna said without much regret in her voice. She knew that much of what had been stolen by the bandits had been taken from the Mexican people of Tubac, and some of those could not afford to lose anything at all. Still, it was better to leave the goods here for the Apaches or the wolves or the elements and get her and her companions back to Tubac.

"Get started, then," Calhoun ordered quietly. When Señorita Luna had hurried off, cotton skirt hem flying, Calhoun went to take another look at the wagons. He grabbed a sizable burning stick from one of the fires for the task. He wanted to find the wagon that needed the least emptying.

He realized that he soon had a small entourage. It would have annoyed him, considering his state of rage anyway, but he knew they were just trying to be helpful. They were scared and relieved, and eager to be away from this dreadful place.

He made his selection, basing it more on the fact that it was the wagon with the two full water barrels than on the amount of goods it had in it. Tossing the stick into the fire, he pointed at two women, then helped them into the bed of the wagon.

"What do we do weeth all these theengs, señor?" one of the two asked in a heavily accented voice.

"Toss 'em."

With something approaching glee, the two women did his bidding. He joined in, tossing out the heavier items, without regard to what they were. As the three cleared room in the wagon bed, another woman, then still another, were assisted up and helped.

In the midst of the work, Señorita Luna arrived and called to Calhoun in the wagon. "Your supper is ready," she said when she had his attention.

He nodded and asked one of the women to hand him a stick to use as a torch. With it held high, he looked around the wagon. "Reckon I got all the heavy stuff, ladies. Y'all finish up here while I eat." He vaulted over the side of the wagon, landing lightly. He pulled his hat off and wiped the sweat from his forehead with the hand that held the hat.

Señorita Luna and Señorita Zbarra served him up some spiced beans and—to his surprise—tamales, plus coffee dosed with mescal. He was pleased with it all and nodded as he dug in.

Finally full, he rolled a cigarette and puffed it while sipping another mug of mescal-laced coffee. He finished and pushed himself reluctantly up. Though still driven by rage and a desire for revenge, the burning of adrenaline had faded to embers.

He checked on the women emptying the wagon, and found they were nearly done. He went to get four of the bandits' mules. When he got them to the wagon, he found that Señorita Lugo had already hauled up most of the harness that would be needed. Calhoun nodded at her.

She was a tall, ungainly woman in her mid-twenties, with broad shoulders and limp hair. Her cheeks were sunken, making her cheekbones seem like twin jutting promontories. A pointed chin and buck teeth didn't help her looks any, although Calhoun found that if he stared into her wide, luminous eyes a bit, he could forget what the rest of her looked like.

She was also a willing worker, and set right in helping him harness the team to the wagon.

Once that was done, Calhoun had most of the other women load what supplies he thought they would need in the back of that wagon. Then he had Señorita Lugo get two of the bandit horses and tie them to the back of the wagon as spares. At the same time, he saddled the sorrel. At the last moment, he tied his pack mule to the back of the wagon, too, in case one of the wagon-pullers came to harm.

Finally he pulled himself into the saddle. He rode over to where the rest of the bandits' horses were still tethered. Without dismounting, he pulled the Bowie, leaned over, and cut the ropes. Most of the animals remained where they were, but Calhoun knew that once they discovered they were unfettered, they would begin drifting off.

He trotted over to the wagon. "You ladies ready?" he asked. When several murmured, *"Sí,"* and the

rest nodded eagerly, Calhoun rode up alongside
Señorita Lugo. "You ready, ma'am?" he asked.

Señorita Lugo nodded, seemingly unconcerned.

"Let's move, then," Calhoun said. He moved up
past the lead mules and then a bit farther. When he
heard the wagon creak and lurch behind him, he set
a slow steady pace, figuring the mules would follow
the sorrel.

It took more than an hour to get to the mouth of
the canyon, and a half an hour or so to go through
the slim opening out of the canyon and get the
wagon turned onto the trail.

Calhoun paused for a few minutes to let the animals
rest. Everyone had a cupful of water, and then they
pushed on again. By dawn's first light, they were in
the valley and on the banks of the mud bog that
might on occasion be a river or stream.

Calhoun looked back. He supposed most of the
women had napped at least a little on the rocky, jolting trail. Still, they looked plumb worn out. The
freshest looking one of the bunch was Señorita
Lugo, whose radiant brown eyes were glowing in the
pink dawn.

"Let's hold up awhile, ladies," Calhoun said, riding
back to the wagon.

"We want to go on," Señorita Luna said defensively.

"The animals need rest, and we need food," Calhoun
said evenly. "We'll pull out soon." He figured that
once the women had gotten off the wagon and
eaten, they would be more than happy to sleep for a
day or two.

He was only partially right. They were willing to

sleep, but most were up in about four hours, preparing another meal and getting ready to leave.

Calhoun, who woke at the first sounds of the others rising, nodded to himself. He got up and they were soon on their way.

Early in the afternoon, three days later, they rolled into Tubac.

CHAPTER

✳ 27 ✳

Calhoun left the women to the cheering, stunned masses of citizens who turned out, and he headed for Goodykoontz's saloon. He dismounted just outside the saloon and looped the reins over the hitching rail. He checked both Dragoons and settled them into his holsters, without the loops over the hammers.

He plunged into the saloon and steamed toward the bar. He had had three days of traveling across the desert with a wagonload of women to let his rage build to a boil again. He had planned to head straight for the office at back, but there was business that had to be taken care of here first.

He stopped at the bar and slammed both palms down on the polished wood surface. Glaring at a frightened bartender, he snapped, "Bring that shotgun out from under the bar and lay it here."

"Yessir." The bartender did as he was told. As the weapon clattered on the wood, the bartender said quietly, "He ain't back there."

"Where is he?" Calhoun demanded in a hissing snarl.

"Don't know. But neither he nor Mr. Perlmutter has been there today, nor most of the past few days."

"You don't mind if I just go back there and check, do you, Mr. Weems?" Calhoun asked rhetorically as he picked up the shotgun. He stared hard into the bartender's eyes. "Now put your hands flat on the bar." After the bartender did, Calhoun turned and began walking away. Two steps later, he looked back over his shoulder. "And leave 'em there."

He strode across the room, unafraid that someone would shoot him in the back. He knew Weems did not carry a pistol, preferring to rely on the scattergun to calm troublesome customers. He also had taken note of everyone in the place when he had entered. None was a threat to him.

He kicked the door open and swept into the room in a rush, Weems's shotgun ready. The room was empty.

He spun and stomped out, stopping at the bar again. Weems still stood with his palms on the wood. Calhoun shoved the muzzle of the shotgun into the juncture of Weems's neck and chin. He cocked both triggers. "Where's Goodykoontz?" he asked tightly.

"I don't know," Weems squawked.

"Where's lard ass's house?" he asked after only a moment's hesitation for thought.

"North toward the arroyo. Just past Docker's and Meyers', go east. It's the last house before the fields. Big place. Can't miss it."

Calhoun pulled the shotgun away, turned, and walked boldly across the saloon and outside into the sweltering heat. He dropped the scattergun into a round wood water trough nearby, and pulled himself into the saddle. The celebration toward the southern part of the town was still going on. He ignored it as he headed north.

Weems had been right this time, too. The house was unmistakable. Though the house was adobe, like every other building in this part of the world, Goodykoontz's had been whitewashed. A white-washed adobe fence about five feet tall surrounded the property. Between the house and fence were chuparosa, mesquite, ironwood, and even tall vines of roses.

Calhoun stopped a little distance away and looked the place over. The house was big and rambling, with real glass in the many windows. A stable and other outbuildings, some of adobe, some of cactus and mesquite, ran out toward the east and the Indian fields.

Calhoun rode into the yard through the adobe arch in the fence, not really caring if anyone saw him from inside the house. He turned to his left and edged close to the house. He moved down the long, low side of the building, peering in windows when he had the chance. He saw nothing.

Continuing his slow ride, he turned around the back of the house. There was nothing much there except piles of rubble and wood and equipment. And a wood fence. He stopped at the end of the gate in the fence and dismounted. He tied the reins to a spiky paloverde tree, and tested the gate. It swung open easily. With a nod, he slid the heavy Greener shotgun out of the saddle scabbard.

The back of the house was oddly shaped. Inside

the gate, to his left, was the adobe wall of a room, that made a right angle to another wall going across in front of him several feet away. The wall took another abrupt turn, creating something of a small alcove before running out to the full length of the building again.

He stepped into the alcove and looked into the window to his left. All he had to see through was a crack in the inside shutters. The room was dimly lit by candles, but it was enough for him to be able to see.

Though she was obscured by Goodykoontz's fat bulk rising off the rickety bed, Calhoun knew without a doubt that it was Lucille. He was sickened at the sight of her limp form, and disgusted with the flabby nakedness of Madison Goodykoontz.

The rage hit him like a mule's kick to the chest, and he had to stand a moment to let it dwindle to an almost manageable level. Then he moved.

He spun, looking like a caged animal. There was no doorway into the room where Goodykoontz, Perlmutter, and at least two other men stood around Lucille's mostly inert form. He could not get a shot off through the crack, at least not with any accuracy. Then he spotted a door in the wall opposite the room where Lucille was. He ran for it, loosening the loops on his pistols as he did. Despite his overpowering rage, he gripped the thought that Lucille was alive. She was probably in bad shape, but she was alive!

He burst into the kitchen, hardly noting the hanging chilies and herbs, the piles of pots, pans, and crockery on wooden cupboards. All he saw was a doorway leading to another room deeper into the house. Figuring it to be the dining room, he ran for it, spurs jingling.

He was in the room in a rush. One swift glance told him the four men sitting in stiff chairs around a dining table were Goodykoontz's gunmen. He jerked the shotgun to his shoulder and fired without really aiming.

The two blasts ripped into three gunmen, killing one and wounding the other two, one of those only slightly.

The fourth man, hampered by the table, was having trouble getting his pistol out. Calhoun charged across the room and smashed the butt of the scattergun into the man's face. The man groaned through his mangled mouth and slumped, hitting his left cheek hard on the wood table.

Calhoun spun and surveyed the room. The one wounded man had died; the other was bleeding heavily from the buckshot holes in his back and side, but was making movements toward a revolver lying on the floor. Without compunction, he kicked the man in the face, then calmly slit his throat with the Bowie.

The man lying half on the table moaned and feebly tried to push himself up. Calhoun moved toward him, blood-dripping knife in one hand, shotgun in the other. He dropped the scattergun on the table with a clunk and then rammed the Bowie home in the man's guts.

Calhoun moved out of the anteroom into a long,

carpeted hallway. He looked through the door across from him and saw a bedroom that smelled powerfully of leather and wood and well-tanned furs, and was filled with rich furnishings. It was devoid of humans.

But the room he wanted was to his left, a few feet away. Dragoon in hand, he charged, slamming into the door. The wood splintered under the power of his fury, and he tumbled into the room. He stopped, still standing, when he hit the bed.

A gun fired, sounding very loud in the small room. Calhoun felt a bullet clip his shirt. In a snarling rage, he spun and fired the Dragoon until it was empty. Between his rage-clouded eyes and the sudden thick cloud of smoke, he could not see much for a few moments. Without thinking, he dropped the Dragoon into his holster and pulled the other one.

The room was eerily quiet, he realized, with only a weak breathing sound to be heard. As the powder smoke cleared, he spotted three bodies lying in various jumbles around the room. None was Goodykoontz.

Slowly Calhoun turned to the bed. Lucille lay there naked. She looked emaciated, and her thin frame was covered with welts, sores, and bruises. She tried to smile, though. "'Bout time you got here," she whispered in a voice that was wrenching in its agony.

"I had business to tend to," Calhoun said lamely. He knelt and took one of her hands in a big, hard paw. He felt like his heart had been torn out when he looked at her. He started to stand. "I best get a doc for you."

"Too late," Lucille whispered feebly, tugging lightly at him.

He knelt again, sliding away the Dragoon. He lifted her upper torso in her arms and then kissed her at her impassioned request. She died that way, in his arms and with his warm mouth on hers. He set her gently back down on the bed, stood, and pulled the covers up over her.

As he turned away, he felt cold inside, with an icy rage sitting in the pit of his stomach. Without really noticing how he saw it, he spotted blood leading to another door. He followed it and entered the big, plush bedroom he had seen from the hall.

Madison Goodykoontz cowered in a corner, his naked blubber quivering. He was a pathetic and disgusting sight. A string of spittle hung from his jiggling lips onto one shaking, fat breast. Blood dribbled down from his left shoulder, and bits of it flecked the left leg.

"Why?" Calhoun asked tightly, eyes narrowed. It was all he could do to keep from blasting the obese wretch of a man.

"Why what?" Goodykoontz asked, dazed eyes on his tormentor.

Calhoun was not taken in by the look. He could see the cunning barely hidden in Goodykoontz's little round eyes, though he knew the man's fear was real, too. He thumbed back the hammer and took deliberate aim at Goodykoontz's crotch.

Goodykoontz's pasty face turned as white as new

snow, and his flabby hands tried to cover his shriveled manhood. "No," he gasped weakly.

"Talk," Calhoun said in a voice as cold as the grave.

"I . . . I can't. I . . . I've got to go . . . to take a leak."

"Go 'head," Calhoun said with a callous shrug.

"But, I . . ."

Calhoun fired and the round lead ball plowed through the expensive rug and into the wood floor two inches from where Goodykoontz's fat hands covered his privates.

Goodykoontz looked like he had just swallowed a porcupine. There came the sound of release, and then the stench of fear-inspired urine soaking the rug.

"You've gone, lard ass. Now talk."

Goodykoontz saw the rage simmering behind Calhoun's narrowed eyes, and he felt a fear he had never even thought possible. "Mr. Nighswander, Blackie, and Four Eyes were supposed to kill you the first time you rode out of here after the bandits," Goodykoontz said, voice strong but shaking. "Mr. Perlmutter wanted a taste . . . a . . . session with . . . her."

"Why?" The word was curt, strangled.

Goodykoontz's fat shoulders rose and fell. "I never could understand Mr. Perlmutter. He has odd notions now and again." He shuddered. "When Mr. Perlmutter and I heard you were back in town, we concocted that story about the bandits—who'd been through here again—taking . . . her."

"How long were you callin' the shots for Sepulveda?"

"You know?" Goodykoontz was more surprised than worried.

"I persuaded one of Sepulveda's men to talk," Calhoun said dryly.

Goodykoontz nodded, acknowledging the information.

"Why'd you have 'em come back through so soon?" Calhoun asked.

"To give Sepulveda's men a little bonus. They had done their jobs well. Nighswander and the other two were supposed to meet up with them after taking care of you. To help them celebrate their successes, I allowed them to take some of the women—the damned Mexican women, of course. I wouldn't let them get anywhere near the white women." He had spoken matter-of-factly, as if such a thing was simply a matter of course.

Calhoun nodded. He could see the sense of it all. Since Nighswander, Blackie, and Four Eyes had failed at their job in killing him, sending him chasing after the bandits again would seem almost guaranteed to end up with him dead, or so Goodykoontz would think.

"You've been abusin' Lucille all this time?"

Goodykoontz shrugged, sending up an avalanching cascade of vibrating flesh. "Mr. Perlmutter spent most of the time with her, though, of course, the other men wanted their share."

"And you?" Calhoun asked, his voice unrelenting in its hatred.

"We all have our weaknesses, Mr. Calhoun," Goodykoontz said. He seemed to have gotten over his fear, being lost in some other world. "Women have never taken to me, for obvious reasons. Even my whores." He sighed. "Once was usually more than enough with them. I learned to leave them alone, or they would be of no use in making money." The mountain of flesh quivered again. "So I must partake when I can."

Calhoun could see no reason to let this fat bag of wind and revulsion live any longer.

C H A P T E R

⋆ 28 ⋆

Calhoun headed out of the room, into the hallway, leaving Goodykoontz sitting on the floor in his bedroom. He went into the dining room right across from the bedroom and picked up his shotgun off the table. He loaded it with powder and ball taken from the pouch at his waist.

Laying the scattergun back on the table, he then reloaded both Dragoons, using already loaded cylinders from the hard-leather pouch. Rearmed, he went into the hallway again and looked into the bedroom.

Goodykoontz was still alive, sitting in a growing pool of blood. His flabby, ghostly white corpus was decorated with five bullet wounds, none in a particularly lethal spot. Most of his teeth were scattered about on his fat gut or on the floor nearby. His mouth was a mass of blood and broken teeth stumps in a pattern that corresponded to the toe of Calhoun's bloody right boot. Goodykoontz also was missing most of his nose as well as both ears. Calhoun had considered continuing lopping off other parts of Goodykoontz's anatomy, but decided he did not have the time, seeing as how he wanted to get after Harry Perlmutter.

Calhoun glanced toward the door of the smaller bedroom, the one where Lucille's body lay, and his vision blurred with the rage that boiled up anew. He pulled a Dragoon and calmly shot Goodykoontz twice more, low in the gut. The balls found no vitals, but would be fatal nonetheless. It would be a slow, agonizing death, too.

Calhoun set the shotgun on the bed and patiently reloaded the two empty chambers of the Dragoons, using paper cartridges. He never took his eyes off of Goodykoontz while he worked, somehow enjoying the agonizing glaze in Goodykoontz's eyes.

As Calhoun dropped the revolver in his holster, he stepped up close to Goodykoontz. He spit on Goodykoontz's face. "Die in agony, you fat piece of shit," he muttered. He turned and headed into the smaller bedroom. He could not bring himself to look at Lucille's blanket-covered body as he slipped out the side door.

He stopped outside, looking around. He knew Perlmutter had come this way; Goodykoontz had told him so, while Calhoun had encouraged him to talk. There were several gates in the adobe wall that surrounded the house and yards. One, near the stable, was open. Calhoun headed for it.

Perlmutter was nowhere around the house. Calhoun was not sure where Goodykoontz's former guard had gotten off to, so Calhoun headed toward town. He figured Perlmutter most likely would be there, trying to drum up some help, unless he had taken one of Goodykoontz's horses and lit out. Calhoun had seen no indication that he had.

People were still gathered around Sepulveda's wagon, as Calhoun strode past. He did not stop when someone called out, "Señor Calhoun."

Juan Sosa watched Calhoun. Señorita Luna moved up beside him. "All I wanted to do was to thank him for helping," Sosa said quietly.

"There is something wrong, Señor Sosa," Señorita Luna said, watching Calhoun. Suddenly she gasped. "Look," she said, pointing.

Up ahead, five gunmen stepped out of Goodykoontz's saloon, followed by Perlmutter. The latter halted on the wood walk under the portico in front of the saloon. The others moved into the street and, upon seeing Calhoun moving closer to them, fanned out, waiting.

Calhoun stopped about twenty yards from the five. "Move, or die, boys," Calhoun said in tight, angry tones.

"No," Perlmutter said haughtily from his perch on the porch, "it is you who will die, Mr. Calhoun. To pay for all the trouble you have caused."

"What trouble?" Calhoun asked innocently. He heard sounds of people moving up behind him, but the sounds did not sound threatening. He could not afford to look in any case. That might give the five gunmen too much of an opening.

"The murder of Madison Goodykoontz," Perlmutter said glibly. "The murder of several of Mr. Goodykoontz's employees. The murder . . . of Lucille Viejo." He fought back a smile of triumph.

There were some gasps from behind Calhoun.

"Goodykoontz ain't dead," Calhoun said flatly.

Despite his fury, he kept himself in check. He wanted others to know that he was innocent, not for any notion of self-preservation but to ensure that Perlmutter died. Once Perlmutter was dead, Calhoun didn't much care if he died.

Perlmutter looked shocked at the words.

"Of course, you wouldn't know that, you son of a bitch, since you were runnin' your ass off to get out of Goodykoontz's house, leaving all the bodies behind."

"You weave a wonderful pack of lies," Perlmutter responded evenly, though it did little to mask his growing fear.

"Tellin' the truth'd go a long ways to your eternal rest bein' peaceful," Calhoun said. "Especially about Señora Viejo."

"You've overstayed your welcome, Calhoun," Perlmutter said, trying to regain control.

"What happened to Señora Viejo?" someone called from the crowd. Other voices concurred.

"She was killed in a fit of jealous rage by that son of a bitch," Perlmutter said unctuously, pointing at Calhoun.

"She died after a couple weeks of abuse and torture by you and that walkin' pile of pig shit you kissed the ass of every day." Calhoun's eyes burned with the rage within him, and his lips were tight with it.

"Lying bastard," Perlmutter said, but his face gave him away to all who looked. "Kill him!"

As the five gunmen went for their pistols, a shot rang out from just behind and to the left of Calhoun. One of the five went down.

Calhoun had one of his Dragoons out and popped off a shot, hitting one of the gunmen in the leg. He cranked his head left, trying to find out where the other shot had come from, but a mass of people surged forward, rushing toward the gunmen around both sides of Calhoun.

He stood there a moment, watching in some surprise the Mexicans who not long ago had still been celebrating the return of the women captured by the bandits. Even the women had joined them. Two were shot down as they swarmed over the gunmen.

Calhoun ran for the saloon as he spotted Perlmutter bolting into it. He barged straight into the saloon, figuring Perlmutter would not expect that, and even if ready would have a hard time hitting a moving target.

Perlmutter must've been anticipating him, since a ball barely missed him as he ripped through the door.

Just inside, Calhoun swerved left, heading for the side of the bar. Two shots rang out, hitting adobe behind him. He stopped and peered around the corner of the bar. Perlmutter stood with a smoking pistol in his hand.

Calhoun popped up and vaulted over the bar, landing inside in a crouch. A bullet crashed into bottles above, sending a cascade of glass down over his head and back. He grabbed a bottle and flung it up and over the bar. A shot rang out.

Calhoun moved a bit farther down the bar, grabbed another bottle, and tossed it. Again a shot was fired. Calhoun was not sure Perlmutter had fired all the shots since he had burst into the room, but he figured it was so. In his quick glance at the room as he charged inside, Calhoun had seen only half a dozen patrons, none of whom usually carried a gun.

Calhoun came up fast, slapping his arms across the bar, Dragoon cocked and ready. He saw Perlmutter frantically trying to reload his cap-and-ball pistol, no easy task under the best of circumstances.

"Drop the piece, Perlmutter," Calhoun ordered.

Perlmutter did not answer. He was sure Calhoun would kill him if he was unarmed. He was not about to let that happen.

The few patrons of the saloon, as well as the bartender, whom Calhoun had found cowering behind the bar, headed for the door as quickly as possible.

Calhoun took his time aiming, and then he fired. The pistol flew out of Perlmutter's hands, clattering on the floor.

Perlmutter clutched one hand with the other, looking in horror as Calhoun came around the end of the bar.

As Calhoun headed slowly toward Perlmutter, letting his rage reach the right temperature, he dropped the revolver into the holster. He figured that a gunshot was too good for a man like Harry Perlmutter. No, he wanted to do this close up.

Perlmutter suddenly swept up a bottle from the table next to him and swung it at Calhoun's head. Calhoun snaked out his left hand and blocked the blow with his forearm. As the bottle crashed to the floor, Calhoun punched Perlmutter on the underside of the joint where arm met shoulder.

Perlmutter groaned as pain raced down the length of his arm. He grabbed the joint with his left hand.

Calhoun slid out the big Bowie. "You miserable bastard," Calhoun said hatefully. He plunged the blade deep into Perlmutter's stomach and ripped it left and right and upward. He pulled the knife out and stepped back.

Perlmutter looked down and moaned. The pain was sharp, biting, almost exquisite in its brilliance. He glanced up at Calhoun, not fully comprehending his plight. He was more amazed at the moment at the icy sensation in his guts than he was afraid.

Calhoun strolled to the bar and picked up a towel used to wipe the wood surface. He cleaned the blade and slid it away. He watched as Perlmutter stumbled unthinkingly toward the door. Calhoun grabbed a bottle and pulled the cork with his teeth. He spit the cork out and swallowed a healthy dose of whiskey. Pulling out his fixings, he rolled a smoke and fired it up. Then he followed Perlmutter.

Perlmutter had staggered outside. The people, who had gathered just off the portico after taking care of the five gunmen, gasped almost as one. There was something frightful about a well-dressed man coming out of a saloon holding in his hands the billowing, snakelike mass of his intestines where they spilled out of his gaping abdomen.

Perlmutter sank to his knees and then pitched forward on his face.

Calhoun came out of the saloon, cigarette in one hand, bottle of whiskey in the other. He felt cold and dead inside. He stepped up and, using the toe of one boot, rolled Perlmutter over on his back. Goodykoontz's right-hand man was dead.

Calhoun stood stone-faced as they lowered Lucille Viejo's body, ensconced in the finest coffin in all of Tubac, into the ground. He wasn't sure how he made it through the funeral, but he did. In fact, he couldn't remember a hell of a lot of the past few days.

After killing Perlmutter, he had gone back to Goodykoontz's house. By then, word had spread throughout Tubac, and a number of people were there. Calhoun's landlady, Señora Alvarez, was among them, and she was directing the gentle removal of Lucille's body.

"It is all right, Señor Calhoun," she said, her accent even more pronounced than usual. "I will take care of these things."

"*Gracias,*" Calhoun said. He meant it. He turned and left, still carrying the bottle of whiskey. He figured he would need it.

Señorita Luna was waiting outside the house. "I will stay with you, señor," she said shyly. She had a desperate look of longing in her eyes, but Calhoun was not interested. Not with Lucille's body not even cold yet.

"I'm obliged for the offer, ma'am," he said quietly. "But I ain't fit company for a decent woman right now." He went off to his room at Señora Alvarez's and got roaring drunk, though it took more than the one bottle he had carried with him. It had also taken two pails of Tómas Hidalgo's homemade mescal.

In the morning, he felt horrible with a hangover, but some of Señora Alvarez's good food, plus some odious concoction she had forced him to take, settled his roiling stomach and eased the pain in his head. Then Señora Alvarez told him of the arrangements for Lucille's burial.

He nodded and headed to Sosa's store for a new set of clothes. He figured Lucille deserved that much. He had a bath, too, and then went to the funeral. Señora Alvarez stood at his left, a nervous, tentative Señorita Luna to his right. The latter kept a good grip on his right arm.

Afterward, he promised Señorita Luna that he would call on her a little later that afternoon. She left happy, and Calhoun walked to the stables, where he gathered up his flaxen sorrel horse and walked it back to Señora Alvarez's house. He saddled the animal and packed his few belongings.

As he pulled himself into the saddle, Señora Alvarez handed him a sack of food. She had known all along he would be leaving, and saw no need to say anything. She merely smiled sadly up at him and nodded.

Moments later he rode out of Tubac, heading north, an ache in his chest.

CLINT HAWKINS is the pseudonym of a newspaper editor and writer who lives in Phoenix, Arizona.

Saddle-up to these

THE REGULATOR by *Dale Colter*
Sam Slater, blood brother of the Apache
and a cunning bounty-hunter, is out to
collect the big price on the heads of the
murderous Pauley gang. He'll give them
a single choice: surrender and live, or go
for your sixgun.

THE REGULATOR—Diablo At Daybreak
by *Dale Colter*
The Governor wants the blood of the
Apache murderers who ravaged his
daughter. He gives Sam Slater a choice:
work for him, or face a noose. Now
Slater must hunt down the deadly rene-
gade Chacon…Slater's Apache brother.

THE JUDGE by *Hank Edwards*
Federal Judge Clay Torn is more than a
judge—sometimes he has to be the jury
and the executioner. Torn pits himself
against the most violent and ruthless
man in Kansas, a battle whose final ver-
dict will judge one man right…and one
man dead.

THE JUDGE—War Clouds
by *Hank Edwards*
Judge Clay Torn rides into Dakota where
the Cheyenne are painting for war and
the army is shining steel and loading
lead. If war breaks out, someone is
going to make a pile of money on a river
of blood.